A Secret Visitor to Saltmarsh Quay

Ian Wilfred

A Secret Visitor to Saltmarsh Quay
Copyright © 2017 by Ian Wilfred

This is a work of fiction. Names, characters, places and incidents are used fictitiously and any resemblance to persons living or dead, business establishments, events, locations or areas, is entirely coincidental.

No part of this work may be used or reproduced in any manner without written permission of the author, except for brief quotations and segments used for promotion or in reviews.

ISBN: 978 1979434980

Cover Design: Avalon Graphics
Editing: Nancy Callegari
Proofreading: Maureen Vincent-Northam
Formatting: Rebecca Emin
All rights reserved.

Also by Ian Wilfred

Putting Right The Past

The Little Terrace of Friendships

For Ron

Acknowledgements

There are a few people I'd like to thank for getting *A Secret Visitor To Saltmarsh Quay* out into the world.

The fabulous Rebecca Emin at Gingersnap Books for organising everything for me and who also produced both kindle and paperback books. Nancy Callegari for all the time and effort she spent editing the book, Maureen Vincent-Northam for proofreading, and the very talented Cathy Helms at Avalon Graphics for producing the terrific cover.

Finally for my late mum who is always with me in everything I do.

Chapter 1

As David walked up the hill to the hotel he started to realise it would only be a week or so before walking to work would be over for the winter. Soon the weather would change and he'd have to start driving every day. Although the walk only took thirty minutes, it was something he would really miss but there was no sense in getting wet and windswept first thing every morning. Once around the final bend in the cliff path, there it was; the stunning Saltmarsh Cliff Hotel and the first thing that came to mind every time he saw it was how blessed he was to work in such a beautiful location. He felt so happy, yet something in the back of his mind told him he should be sad and depressed with everything that had gone on in his life over the last few months. However, he couldn't change the past and he needed to move on. Life, he thought, is far too short to feel sorry for yourself.

"Good morning, Glenda. How are you today? Is there anything I need to know before I pop into the breakfast room?"

"No, I don't think so. Everyone turned up for duty. There are only four check outs and three check-ins today. There's a party of ten booked in the Orangery for lunch at midday for a retirement presentation. The flowers have arrived and the group have hired the room until four o'clock. The only other thing is that I had an email from a PA in America wanting to book a telephonic appointment with you. I haven't replied as I wanted to check with you first."

"I didn't really need to come in today as you've got everything organised. What would I do without you? This is why you've won the title of 'Head Receptionist of the Year' in our part of the United Kingdom, Glenda. Everyone should have a Glenda in their life."

"It's just that I like to be organised. There's really no hidden secret to it, just plan, check and deliver. Coming back to the email though, what time shall I book the phone call for, Mr Rose?"

"I think around four o'clock as housekeeping will have finished and I need to spend an hour or so with them today. Thank you."

"Good morning. Everything all right with your breakfast today, Mrs Clime?"

"Oh, Mr Rose, you don't have to keep asking me that every day. In all the years I've been staying at the Saltmarsh Cliff Hotel I've not eaten anything which hasn't been cooked to perfection. I was just saying to Clare that I remember when she first started here and now look at her. In just a few years she's now the Restaurant Manager. The staff you employ are so friendly and helpful. By the way, I've had a chat to Glenda and she's booked me in for a week at Christmas as I cannot think of anywhere else I would like to celebrate the festive celebrations."

"With all the times you stay with us, I'll soon be putting you on the rota, Mrs Clime. Well, I must get off. Have a lovely day. It's not too cold out there, so you should be able to take a little walk."

"What are you up to today, Mr Rose?"

"Oh, I'm off to find Annie as we're going to be discussing toilets and plumbing. A really exciting day ahead!"

Annie was another of David's favourite members of staff. She had been the Head Housekeeper from the very beginning, the first person he had hired and she treated the hotel as if it was a precious jewel. Nothing was too much trouble for her and every member of staff loved her. She was the hotel 'Mum', always there with a listening ear and advice for all the younger staff.

"Morning, Annie. Are you ready to talk drains and plumbing?"

"No, not today, David as it's all been sorted out. I've had a meeting with Eric, and his friend has advised him how to resolve the problem, so we'll take it from there."

"Annie, I'm not needed in this hotel as both you and Glenda are running the place!"

"No, David, You run the hotel and we manage our departments. We only do the job we're paid to do. Talking of which, I must get on as I'm expecting the linen delivery any time now. Have a lovely day."

The linen delivery was late and as Annie sat

looking out over the grounds of the hotel waiting for its arrival she started pondering about how fortunate she had been after the sudden death of her husband. This job was a life saver. She wasn't ashamed to say it, but the hotel was a replacement for her beloved Jim. Some people look for another partner after a bereavement, but not Annie. The love that she and Jim had for each other could never be replaced by anyone else. This job was far more than a means of earning a living, the hotel and the staff were her life.

***

David sat at his desk waiting for the call from America. He could see a couple of fishing boats out on the horizon and he smiled to himself. Although he had worked in some of the finest hotels in the country as well as in France, the Saltmarsh Cliff Hotel was certainly his favourite. From the time he was head hunted to be part of the exciting new venture, he knew this was going to be very special. It would not just be another job, but the beginning of a new life for him and his wife – now sadly his ex wife. The hotel and the staff were his family and in a strange way he needed the hotel more than it needed him He recognised that it was also the same for Annie as the hotel had become her new life following the death of her husband. "Good afternoon; David Rose, General Manager of The Saltmarsh Cliff Hotel. How can I help you today?"

"Hello, Mr Rose. My name is Connie Lamont and I'm interested in booking your best suite of rooms for six to eight weeks for a client of mine. Firstly though, I need to confirm a lot of details regarding the location, the rooms, the staff, etc."

It was nearly two hours later when David and Miss Lamont ended their conversation. David felt elated, not only because of the exciting booking but because it was the first time in a while that he had talked in great depth about The Saltmarsh Cliff Hotel. He had been able to explain how it had been a dilapidated 50 bedroom hotel and how the company had bought it and spent millions on refurbishing it into a 22 luxury suite five-star establishment. He was so proud of the staff he had employed from the head chef right down to the fabulous housekeeping team.

David was pleased he had taken notes during his conversation with Miss Lamont. The booking would be a very profitable one for the hotel, but looking back over the details and analysing the situation, he wondered whether he and the staff would be able to cope with the new guest and her requirements.

An eminent American female was undergoing surgery and coming to recuperate at The Saltmarsh Cliff Hotel from December through to the end of January. It was important that no one would know about this or see her, as she would stay in her rooms. Organising meals and the daily cleaning of the rooms would be handled through her PA, Miss

Lamont. Every member of staff would have to sign a confidentiality statement just in case they were to discover the identity of the mystery guest. This booking would be worth a lot of money to the hotel over the Christmas period.

David came to the conclusion that this guest must be very famous and wondered how he could keep her name a secret from the staff and also the village. As for the operation she was recuperating from, that in itself would have the staff guessing.

Chapter 2

It had been several weeks since that initial conversation with Miss Lamont, but the day had dawned for the mystery guest to arrive. David still didn't have a clue who she was, but he had agreed to all Miss Lamont's demands. The staff had all signed legal documents from the guest lawyer and the only thing he had insisted on was a name for the guest; he wasn't having her referred to as 'mystery guest' through her entire stay. She was to be known as Miss Spring, a name chosen by herself. Her rooms were ready. Eight suitcases had arrived the previous day and everything which had been requested, from flowers to magazines, were already in her rooms. All David now had to do was await her arrival and get her in the suite without anyone recognising her. He had managed to keep the exact time of her arrival a secret by telling staff that she was due at the hotel the following day, so it was only Glenda and himself who were aware she was arriving that day.

"Glenda, I think we're ready. Housekeeping have all gone, the chefs and kitchen staff won't be back on duty until five o'clock, I've sent Eric and Paul off to the garden centre to get some replacement shrubs for the driveway, so it just leaves you, myself and Clare here. I will get Clare to stay behind the bar, you stay in reception, and I will show Miss

Lamont and Miss Spring up to their suites."

"Mr Rose, I hope you don't mind me asking, but what's your view on all of this? Have you any idea who she is and why she is here?"

"No, Glenda. Those are the questions I should be asking you. You're a woman with a great sense of intuition."

"I think she may be hiding from something and to me, an operation means either a facelift or an abortion. Why else would she not want to be seen, Mr Rose?"

"Oh dear, what have I let us in for? If you're correct and news of who she is and why she's here gets out, it could ruin the reputation of the hotel and put people off coming here. "Oh, God, what have I done?"

A large limousine with blackened out windows pulled up outside the main door. A short female aged around 30 stepped out, followed by a driver in a chauffeur's uniform.

"Hello, I'm Connie. I'm here to see David Rose."

"Good afternoon, I'm David. Everything is ready for you and Miss Spring. There are just a few staff on duty as they have been told you're arriving tomorrow. I will show you to your rooms."

Connie indicated to the chauffeur to open the car door. Glenda and David were both rather nervous and excited at the same time as this was it! After weeks of mysterious preparation, the famous American had arrived. Surely they would be able to get a look at her as there was no way she could get from the car to the rooms without them seeing a glimpse of her face.

"Mr Rose, I must ask you not to acknowledge Miss Spring. Please just lead the way to our rooms."

Glenda realised it was all down to her as with David leading the way she would be the only one to see Miss Spring's face. The car door opened and a very tall female wearing a black cape with a huge hood and a black veil over her face stepped out. Not only could Glenda not see her face, but she couldn't even estimate Miss Spring's age as the cape covered her. David opened the door to the suite, followed by both women. Miss Spring went straight into the bathroom and Connie asked where her rooms were, planning to meet David in reception in half an hour.

"Talk about cloak and dagger, Glenda. Have you ever witnessed anything like that before? I'll say one thing, Glenda, You were spot on with your intuition. As Miss Spring walked past me into the room, the light from the window shone on her face and I could see bandages under her veil."

David and Connie had a chat and she thanked him very much on behalf of Miss Spring, who apparently was extremely grateful for his discretion. The only change to all the arrangements was that there would be a visitor arriving every third day and could they possibly be shown to the suite at around eleven o'clock? David and Glenda discussed this later, both feeling somewhat flat as after all the weeks of excitement building up to arrival of the mystery visitor, it now looked to be an uneventful six weeks before going through the same procedure for her departure.

"So, Glenda, that's that. As from tomorrow we start the Christmas preparations. We have other guests to take care of and a very busy month ahead."

Chapter 3

Ten months earlier in Los Angeles.
Despite all she had been through in her life – not being able to have children, failed marriages, having to pay out millions in divorce settlements, this was one of the few times in her life that Devel had felt so depressed. A constant thing in her life for over 40 years, the thing which had helped to take away the hurt and sadness, was now gone. A half hour meeting with her agent had changed her life forever. Now what should she do?

As she sat in the garden of her beautiful Los Angeles home, Max's words kept coming back to her.

"It's like this, Devel. I'm sorry to say that I can't represent you anymore. I've not managed to get you one single audition for over six months. I know we've worked together for over twenty years, but it's time to call it a day."

"But Max, all actors and actresses experience this. There are thousands of us looking for that one part. Things will improve, I know they will. I've been working since I was four years old, I have a good reputation and the public love me. Just look at the big films and top television shows I've been in. Why give up on me now?"

"Look, Devel, to me you're more than a client. You're my friend and as such I'll be honest with you. I've put your name forward to hundreds of casting directors and they all say the same thing. You've had your day, you're too old."

"Too old." Devel had known and accepted that for a long time, but she didn't want to be like so many of the actresses who had facelift after facelift. People didn't want to see that same pulled look on the faces of actresses. She believed the natural growing old with dignity process was the way to go as she wasn't auditioning for parts suitable for 20-year-olds. What was she going to do? Financially, she didn't need to work, but she had to; it was the one thing in her life which made her get up every day – the hope that another great part was out there for her.

She poured herself another coffee and phoned her best friend, and hairdresser, Mark, who had been her friend for more than 40 years.

"Hi, Mark, it's happened at last. I'm a has-been, not needed anymore, washed up. I've had my fifteen minutes of fame."

"No, darling, forty years of fame and you're not washed up and never will be. I don't know where this talk has come from, but get in your kitchen and start to prepare my favourite dinner and I'll see you at six-thirty."

Devel did just that. She cooked a fabulous meal for them both and they had a lovely evening. As she climbed into bed she felt so much better. She realised that Mark's loyalty was the reason why he was her best friend, but most importantly they had put a plan into action – one which she never imagined would happen, but as far as she was concerned was the only solution.

The next morning, Connie, Devel's PA, got the ball rolling. She would fly over to the UK in December and not return until late January. She loved England and over the years had worked at all the major film studios as the British had always been so kind and friendly towards her. She still couldn't believe that Maddie Main had two facelifts and not one person, either in the press or amongst other actors, had ever guessed. She had retained a normal appearance, since, as Mark had said, she didn't go to the same surgeons who kept turning out the same frozen look on American actresses.

Chapter 4

A week had passed since Miss Spring's arrival at the hotel and she had not been out of her suite. Her only visitor was a middle aged man every third day carrying a big bag. He would stay for about three quarters of an hour and then leave. It was all very discreet. As for Connie, that was a completely different story. She spent a lot of time around the hotel and its grounds, mostly in the afternoons and late evenings, chatting to other guests and being very friendly to the staff. No members of staff had been in Miss Spring's suite as Connie cleaned it herself. Fresh linen and towels were left outside by the housekeeping team.

To be honest, the hotel was so busy preparing for Christmas that the mystery guest in the best suite was of little interest. The staff realised that since Connie guarded her like she was a precious jewel, no one else would ever see her. Being one of the top five-star hotels in Norfolk, they were accustomed to having famous people stay and discretion was always the highest priority.

"Hello, Glenda. Is David here? It's very urgent, I need to speak to him as soon as possible."

"Certainly, Miss Lamont. He's in his office, I'll phone through."

"Please come in and sit down, Miss Lamont. What can I do for you? Is anything wrong?"

"Everything here is fine. Miss Spring Is very happy, but unfortunately I've had a call from America to say that my father has had a stroke and Miss Spring insists that I fly back."

"I'm so sorry to hear that. Have you arranged a flight? Is there anything we can do to help?"

"That's why I'm here. Would you be able to come up to Miss Spring's suite? She's asked to see you, but first of all I need to tell you who Miss Spring really is and why she's here."

Why she was here was not a great surprise. David had seen the bandages on the first day and had guessed the visitor was a doctor, but it was a massive shock to find out who the actress really was. Never in a million years would he have ever guessed it was Devel Devonshire. She had been a huge part of his childhood. They were near enough the same age, so why would such a beautiful woman need a facelift? She had looks which every woman in her age group envied. David had met many famous people, politicians, actors and even royalty. It had never fazed him previously, but meeting Devel under these circumstances made him nervous.

David explained the situation to Glenda, but failed to inform her of the identity of their mystery guest. He took a long look at himself in the mirror, but wasn't exactly sure why. "Pull yourself together, you silly man," he said to himself. "You've met hundreds of well-known people. What's the problem?"

"Please come in and take a seat, David. Miss Devonshire will be joining us shortly."

"Thank you, Miss Lamont."

The bedroom door opened and David could feel his heart beating very fast and the butterflies in his stomach. Come on. Act like a general manager of a hotel, not like a teenage boy, he thought. Devel walked towards him and shook his hand. He was expecting her to be covered in bandages, but there were none, not even a plaster. Her face was red and slightly puffy, but she was stunning. She looked like a film star, because of course she was one.

"Hello, David. It's so nice to meet you properly. First of all, I must say how much I've enjoyed staying here at The Saltmarsh Cliff Hotel. Thank you for the privacy and discretion I've been afforded. I really can't thank you enough. Now we have a little situation which I'm sure can be resolved. It isn't really a problem, just something we need to plan and I'm sure the next few weeks will fly by."

"We are here to do whatever is needed to make your stay private and comfortable, Miss Devonshire."

"Oh, thank you, David. Connie and I have had a chat and the most important thing is that when I leave here in a few weeks, no one needs to know I've been here. I'm more than happy staying in my room looking out to sea. It's not that I don't want to leave the room and explore the beauty of Norfolk, but I'm afraid it's not an option. I won't beat around the bush as I'm sure you are aware why I'm in hiding. You can see for yourself, I've had a little cosmetic surgery."

"Miss Devonshire, your private life is your own business. My staff and I are here to ensure your stay at The Saltmarsh Cliff Hotel is exactly as you wish. If you let me know your requirements for the rest of your stay, I can guarantee we will fulfil your wishes."

"Connie has thought it through and if it is at all possible she suggests it would be best if I only came into contact with one member of staff and also yourself, of course."

"Yes, that's not a problem. It's actually the perfect solution. We just need to give some thought as to who the designated member of staff will be."

"David. I think you have the ideal person to take care of Miss Devonshire already here at the hotel," suggested Connie. "We will obviously pay extra as if they are willing to do this, they will have to work longer hours."

"Who do you have in mind, Connie?"

"David, since we've been here, the person I've had the most dealings with, apart from you and Glenda, is Annie and I think she would care for Miss Devonshire perfectly."

Back at home later in the evening David was reflecting on the day's events. Annie was more than happy to take on the task and to be honest she was the one member of staff who would not be at all star struck. It didn't matter to Annie whether it was royalty or a dustman, if they were a paying guest they would be treated exactly the same. He also felt a little down to think that this beautiful woman who had fame and fortune and was loved by fans all around the world, was unhappy enough to undergo cosmetic surgery. That made him feel quite sad.

It just goes to show that the outside world does not necessarily see the truth. It was similar to his own life. People saw him as a victim, a man whose wife had affairs and had run off with his best friend, but the truth was that after years of putting up with her behaviour, he was now happier than he had been for years.

Chapter 5

Although it was only 10th December, Christmas had already begun at The Saltmarsh Cliff Hotel. The hotel and the tree were both decorated festively and the staff were ready to help the guests celebrate. David and Glenda had spent most of the day going over all the functions booked in to the day before Christmas Eve. Most were from London companies who book anything up to 20 rooms for a few days to have their end of year conferences and treat their staff to a well-deserved break. The hotel did not offer party nights with a disco but fabulous food served in a stunning location. It was one of the hotel's busiest months, making a lot of money, and the staff were prepared for it.

"So, Glenda, that's it. We've crossed the T's and dotted the I's. We just need for it all to start. I don't think we've missed anything out, do you?"

"No. Both the Christmas and New Year packages are fully booked, but I can go over those with you nearer the time. Most of the guests have stayed with us before. The only other thing is Miss Spring. Do we have a date for her departure? I've booked her in until the eighth of January, but with Miss Lamont leaving yesterday, I wondered if there would be any changes."

"I'm not sure. I'll call in on her over the next few days. I'm also seeing Annie later, just to check on how she's getting on with Miss Spring, so leave it with me."

It had been Annie's second day looking after Devel and she found her to be most charming and friendly. They had made general chit chat, neither wanting to overstep the boundaries between guest and employee, but Annie felt very relaxed in the actress's company. When she had cleaned the suite Devel stayed in the bedroom, so she did not feel like she was being watched. The following night would be a bit different as Devel had asked Annie to spend a few hours with her in the evening playing Scrabble, which they both were greatly looking forward to.

David was just going to check that everything was ready for dinner and that the restaurant and kitchen staff were on top form, when he received a call from Marcus, the Director of Operations for the hotel chain. He had planned to come and spend the next day with David and had asked him to clear his diary as there was a lot to chat about. David was not unduly worried about this as Marcus regularly called into the hotel. The only difference was that normally his visits were scheduled in advance. David didn't foresee a problem though, as the hotel was busy and taking good money.

He made sure all the staff were aware of Marcus' visit. They too were not worried since they always gave a hundred and ten per cent. David looked at his watch and saw that it was seven o'clock. Glenda was on duty until eleven, when Ken, the night porter, came on duty so he decided to leave and finish early.

Once home, David poured himself a large glass of wine, put some music on and settled down to do some paperwork. He wanted to be prepared with targets, budgets and the Christmas forecast for the meeting and also wanted to put his plans together for the following year. He was hoping to hold some summer garden parties with marquees on the lawn and thought Marcus would really be in favour of that.

Come ten o'clock and David had finalised everything. Feeling quite pleased with himself he poured another glass of wine. He loved his life – a lovely cottage down near the quay, a job which, if he didn't need the money he would do for free, staff who were more than employees, they were friends. What more did he need in his life? Certainly not another relationship, that was for sure. As he pulled the curtains he could see the lights of a fishing boat way out to sea. That's real work, he thought to himself, out in all weathers trying to earn a living. His life was a doddle compared to that although he had worked hard to get to where he was, spending many years turning run down and troubled hotels into successful businesses. It was now time to slow down and enjoy beautiful Norfolk and his very blessed life.

David was back at the hotel by 6.15. He had a

quick chat with Ken and then went to the kitchen for a large pot of coffee. Sitting at his desk he really didn't know why he was so early. Everything was ready for Marcus. All David had to do was wait for his ten o'clock arrival. He heard Annie come down the corridor and thought that she was also early, but then remembered that she had to take Devel's breakfast up to her by seven o'clock. David had put Devel to the back of his mind and smiled to himself. We have one of the most famous women in the world staying here and I just take it to be the norm. There was a knock at the office door.

"Come in. Good morning, Annie. How are you? Is everything going well with Miss Spring? It's not causing you too much extra work, is it? Do you have time for a quick chat?"

"Go on then. I'm early for Miss Spring. Anyway, it's all going fine thanks, but between you and me, I keep asking myself why?"

"I know what you mean, Annie, so do I. I really don't understand it. She has everything in the world —money, a career, she looks stunning, but she's obviously unhappy."

"Exactly. It's so sad, but we are only here to make sure the guests are looked after and served correctly. It's not for us to comment on their lives. Can I ask you something, David? Is everything all right here at the hotel because it's not like Marcus to come for a visit at such short notice."

"Glenda and I wondered about that, but if

anything is wrong, we'll know about it in a couple of hours, Annie."

"Right. I'd best get on. It's nearly time for Miss Spring's breakfast tray. I hope everything goes well today. I'm sure there's nothing wrong. Marcus probably only wants to check everything is in order for Christmas."

Devel had been awake for hours. For the first time since arriving at the hotel she was feeling trapped and she didn't like it. She was an independent, successful woman, who had been shut away in a suite of rooms for weeks at her own volition. Even if she decided to go back to the States she would be photographed at the airport or on the plane. What a great Christmas scoop that would be for the press. No, she had to stick it out. How many people dream of staying in a five-star hotel over Christmas being waited on hand and foot?

"Good morning, Annie. How are you today?"

"I'm fine, Miss Spring, thank you. How are you?"

"To be honest, I'm fed up to the back teeth. It's only the stunning views that are stopping me from screaming. I've only known you for two days, Annie, but you come across as so contented and happy with your life and that must be such a lovely thing. I really can't believe what I've put myself through these last few weeks, all in the hope that I will get an acting job. I must be mad."

"Miss Spring..."

"Oh, please call me Devel, Spring was just a

stupid name I came up with. I thought spring was fresh and new as the gardens come to life after a cold wet winter, and that's what I thought I was doing, having a new fresh start. Sadly, a little surgery doesn't make things new."

Annie stayed up listening to Devel for over an hour. She had been so open with her, telling her the whole story of losing her agent and Paul talking her into having the surgery. It was such a sad story, and the first thing Annie thought was how could she help her. As she walked to the housekeeping office, one of the chambermaids was coming towards her in her big parka coat. Her hood was up and although Annie couldn't see her face, it did give her an idea. She turned round, went back up to Devel's suite and after a bit of persuading finally Devel agreed that she and Annie would leave the hotel for a little walk down the cliff path to a secluded beach at the bottom. No one would be around as it was mid-December. With the big coat and sunglasses she would just look like someone wrapped up warmly for the winter. They agreed that Annie would come back up to the room at 12 and they could leave by the staff entrance at the back of the hotel.

"Hello, Glenda. How are you today? It's so nice to be back in beautiful Norfolk, with the peace and quiet."

"I know, Marcus. We're very lucky. How was your journey and did you need a room for tonight? I have reserved your favourite one just in case, but I'm afraid it can only be for tonight as we are fully booked from tomorrow right up until the first week of January."

"I'm not sure yet. It depends on how I get on today. Is David in his office?"

"Yes. Go through and I'll get some coffee and homemade Norfolk biscuits sent in."

Glenda considered that to be a strange thing to say. If everything was going well with the hotel, why would he have said that? Something was the matter. She had been in the hotel industry long enough to know that something was about to happen.

"Morning, David. It's so good to be back. Tell me what's been happening. How's Christmas shaping up?"

After about an hour David had gone over the forecast and the budgets and Marcus was more than pleased. He then started to tell Marcus about the planned garden parties and a few other things for the following year, but Marcus wasn't interested. He cut him off and nipped to the toilet. David thought to himself "Why is he here if he doesn't want to know about our future plans? He could have found all the other information from the computer in his London office.

On his return, Marcus faced the hotel manager. "David, you're not daft. Why am I here? I expect you, Glenda and Annie have already asked yourselves that question. Well, it's like this. I have some very exciting news for all three of you."

Marcus opened his briefcase and took out a folder from which David could see drawings and photographs. He also noticed that Marcus appeared to be slightly nervous. Was the hotel having an extension? It was something that had been talked about over the years, but getting the planning permission would be a big problem.

"Let me explain, David. I know you're going to be just as excited about this as I am."

***

Annie led Devel down the back stairs and into the staff corridor, having made sure no one was around. Once out of the hotel, Devel stopped to breathe in the cool, clean, fresh air.

"Oh, Annie. This is just what I need, a crisp and clean British winter. Thank you so much."

As they walked through the garden to the cliff path all they could hear were the sea birds out looking for food. Slowly they made their way down the winding path, silently stopping to take in the stunning views. Annie worried whether she had done the right thing. What would happen if Devel slipped and hurt herself? She would have to get help and the whole village would find out about the world famous actress.

"Oh, Annie. This is so beautiful. Thank you so much. I can't believe how much better I feel already. Oh, look down there. Can we get to that rock? I would so love to sit and just listen to the waves coming in."

"Of course we can. It's quite safe as the tide doesn't come as far as that rock. I call it my special place."

Annie told Devel about the weeks after Jim's death and how she'd come down here in the afternoons to sit on the rock and talk to him. Sometimes walking down she would feel confused and lonely, but after just half an hour sitting and looking out to sea, everything would become clear and the weight would be lifted from her shoulders, ready to face the world again.

"You see, Devel. I could have just given in and become bitter and twisted. Jim wouldn't have wanted that though. He would have said, 'Annie, I've gone, but you have to carry on. Enjoy the rest of your life. None of us know when our time is up.' I've made a new life for myself now, the hotel and my colleagues have become my life or should I say they are my family."

After an hour they strolled back up the cliff path to the hotel. Devel said she was ready for a hot chocolate and a little doze, preferring to give the evening game of Scrabble a miss. She also wanted to order a few things on the Internet. Annie didn't mind at all. She was just so thankful that Devel was feeling better within herself.

Chapter 6

It was 4.30 am and David had hardly slept. He had only been in bed for a few hours as Marcus' visit had left him with such a dilemma. His head was telling him one thing but his heart another. As he pulled back the curtain it was still pitch black but he could see a couple of fishing boats in the distance. Oh, how he loved waking up in Saltmarsh Quay. He had never loved living anywhere so much and never had he loved his life as much as he did now.

"Good morning, Ken. Everything all right?"

"Oh, hello, Mr Rose. You startled me there for a minute. You're very early today. The breakfast chef hasn't arrived yet. Is everything okay?"

"Yes. Everything's good, thanks. Just got a pile of paperwork to get through and it's easier to get it done before the phone starts ringing."

Coffee made, and sat at his desk, David realised that he could have done the paperwork at home. *What did I think I would achieve by coming in so early* he asked himself. He was glad Marcus didn't stay overnight and was also pleased that it was Glenda's day off. He had a lot to think about. Just as everything was so damn perfect in his life, it was all going to change. But it could be changing for the better.

Devel had also been up for hours and had ordered a full cooked English fry up. Annie was quite surprised when the kitchen called her to take the tray up as this was different from her normal fresh juice and muesli.

"Hello, Annie. How are you today? It looks like another fresh crisp morning out there."

"Yes, I do think it's a bit colder this morning, but no sign of any rain. Thank goodness."

As Devel ate her breakfast, Annie cleaned the bathroom, which took next to no time as Devel was such a clean and tidy guest.

"Annie, when you get a minute, I want to tell you my exciting news."

"I'm all ears. Have you been offered an acting role?"

"No, nothing like that, but yesterday after our walk I came back and ordered some things online. Fingers crossed they will be here today. You see, Annie, I'm going to have a little adventure."

Devel went on to explain that since she'd had such a lovely walk the previous day she had decided to order a big coat like the one she had borrowed and also a couple of wigs and some glasses."

"You see, Annie. I'm an actress who is used to playing different characters, so that's what I'll do. For the rest of my stay I'm going to disguise myself, so I can go walking. It's winter; there are not many people around so it should be quite easy."

Annie was slightly concerned as if Devel were to be recognised, it would be her fault because she was the one who had encouraged her to go out.

However, the actress was a grown woman and obviously it was her own decision. Devel had told Annie that she didn't require her for the rest of the day, so she headed back to the housekeeping office to check that everything was running smoothly without her. She didn't really have to ask, as she had a reliable team who knew exactly how things should be run.

David was becoming tired of pondering what to do, so decided he ought to discuss it with someone. He phoned Glenda to see if she had any plans for her night off, and as that she was free he invited her to his cottage for dinner. He then went to look for Annie to see if she was available, and as Devel didn't need her, she too was free. A stop off at the village store on the way home, food and wine bought, and David already felt better in himself.

Glenda and Annie weren't daft. They knew that the evening at David's had to be about Marcus' visit. They arrived promptly at 7.00pm, and had a chat, although Annie and David had to be careful about what they were saying as Glenda was still unaware of Miss Spring's real name.

David cooked a huge cottage pie, real winter comfort food, the wine was flowing and they were having a lovely evening. David had to spoil it by telling Annie and Glenda Marcus' news as it involved them and Marcus was expecting him to have discussed it with them both before their next meeting in London in two days' time.

"Down to business. Why was Marcus in Norfolk yesterday?"

"You don't have to tell us if it's private, David. Glenda and I will understand."

"The thing is, Annie, it does involve all of us."

David then went on to explain almost word for word what Marcus had said. The hotel company had bought up a run down hotel in London and wanted to convert it into a five-star deluxe hotel very similar to The Saltmarsh Cliff. At present it had approximately 90 bedrooms, but after the conversion there would be around 45 suites. It was a very exciting project, but the drawback was that The Saltmarsh Cliff Hotel would have to be sold to fund the work.

"But David, we're making good money for the company. Why would they want to dispose of one of their best assets?"

"You have answered the question yourself, Glenda. Our hotel has gone from a run down three-star to a deluxe five-star in such a short time they can get a top price for it."

Marcus had not been there to talk about The Saltmarsh Cliff Hotel. The new London hotel was on the table and he wanted David to be the General Manager. Not only that, he wanted Glenda and Annie to move as well. After all, it was the three of them working together which had made the Norfolk hotel so successful.

"Oh, David, I can answer that right away. It's not

for me. If I was twenty or thirty years younger I might have given it some thought. I know things might change here, but I love Saltmarsh Quay so much and it would be like moving and leaving Jim behind. My life is here in Norfolk."

"How about you, Glenda? What are your thoughts on the move?"

"If I were to put my career head on, yes it would be the perfect move for me, but like Annie my heart is here in Norfolk. However, I'll give it some thought and talk it over with my friends and family."

The rest of the evening was very light hearted with no in-depth talk about the London move and to David's surprise neither women asked him what he wanted to do. He felt a lot better telling them and since Marcus had first told him about it he knew there was no way that Annie would even contemplate moving. David was keeping an open mind and would go to London to have a look at the area and the hotel as perhaps this was what he needed, time to get away from Norfolk and start a fresh challenge. He had become very set in his ways, so yes, this could possibly be the answer.

The next morning David didn't rush to get to the hotel but instead walked around Saltmarsh. It was quiet, there were no holiday makers and just a few locals out with their dogs, and mothers driving back after having taken the children to school. Could he swap all this for London? Would his job be secure once the hotel was sold? It might not even be a hotel. A rich family might buy it and have it as a holiday home. Perhaps no one's jobs would be safe. There were so many unanswered questions.

David was not the only one with unanswered questions. Back at the hotel Devel was up early and going through her emails. Lots of her friends had been wondering where she was and what was she up to. She sent the same reply to all of them, that she was having a little holiday with friends. However, there was one email that really upset her. It was from Max. He had got her an acting job in a commercial and it would pay good money. Throughout her career she had never done a commercial. She hadn't needed the money and to her it felt like her career was flagging. The bit which really upset her was the product was not for perfume or expensive watches but bleach. She could just see herself in a bathroom squirting the stuff down a toilet. Oh no, that's never going to happen.

With that there was a knock on the door. Annie had arrived with her breakfast tray.

"Morning, Annie. How are you today?"

"Good morning, Devel. I'm fine, thank you. It's a little bit crisper out there today, but there's no rain forecast."

"Oh, good. I'm expecting some parcels today and the companies have said that the deliveries should be before lunch time. If they do come, Annie, I will need them as soon as possible. Could you see to that for me?"

"Of course. Is there anything else you require me to do today?"

"No, Annie, I'm fine. Just the parcels please."

When David finally got to the hotel it was quite busy. A group of business ladies were having a conference day and there were several lorries delivering food and wine. There was also a courier carrying several parcels to reception and Annie was signing for them.

"Morning, Annie. What's all this? Deliveries have to go to the service entrance, not here."

"No, it's all right. These are for Miss Spring. She requires them the minute they arrive, so I'm going to take them right up to her suite."

"I'll give you a hand. There's loads of them."

Devel eyed her parcels. "Oh, thank you both. It's like Christmas. I'm rather excited."

"Do you need help unpacking them?"

"Oh no, I'm fine. You're both very busy. I can manage these and hopefully see you both shortly."

Devel could not wait to open the packages. There were boots, big coats, hats, scarves and jumpers. She wondered whether she had gone over the top and ordered too much. After all, how many thick coats did she really need? She had left the parcel which she was really looking forward to opening until last, as this was the one that would really put her plan into motion. Wigs. Yes, five of them in different colours and styles.

Neither David nor Annie mentioned the sale of the hotel. Glenda was on duty until the afternoon shift, so it just felt like a normal day. David was hoping that tomorrow would hurry up and come as he just wanted to get to London and see whether his gut reaction would be one of excitement or doom and gloom.

Annie spent the rest of the morning carrying out mundane housekeeping jobs and catching up on things. She was just checking the dining room after all the lunch guests had left and noticed someone walking towards her. As she turned, a voice said to her:

"Hello, Annie. What do you think? Am I suitably dressed for a little walk?"

"Good afternoon, Miss Spring. Yes, you certainly are. Have a lovely walk, but just remember the temperature starts to drop at around three o'clock, so I would make sure you're back by then."

As Devel smiled and walked away, Annie thought that no one would ever recognise her. It wasn't just the change in her physical appearance which Annie had noticed, but Devel's attitude. She was more confident and far less fragile, and it had nothing to do with going for a walk. Devel was doing what she loved most of all, the thing which made her breathe. She was playing a part. This was an acting role for her.

Chapter 7

David looked at his watch. In just another thirty minutes the train would be pulling into London. He was so pleased that he had caught the first one of the day as he didn't want to rush getting to the meeting. Time to check out the other hotels in the area and have a few strong coffees first. The one thing he did know was that the ball was firmly in his court. He was ready with questions and his request if he did decide to take the job as it had to work for him one hundred per cent.

As he walked through the door of the hotel two hours later he could feel himself getting excited. Its shabby, run down appearance looked like nothing had been done to the building since the 70s, but God, what potential it had. The company would need to spend millions on it to achieve the five- star rating they wanted and David realised why they would have to sell The Saltmarsh Cliff Hotel to fund the project.

The first two hours were spent with Marcus and the Project Manager. Together they walked every inch of the building. David could clearly see the vision, which was certainly not a quick refit. The hotel had to be taken back to the bare bones and this would take a long time to complete. Once all the partitions and stud walls had been removed it would be back to the original huge rooms with their high ceilings and fabulous windows.

After the tour it was time to get down to the nitty gritty. Marcus had booked a table for lunch at a very exclusive restaurant where they were joined by two of the other directors. There was lots of discussion about the marvellous job David had done in Norfolk and how much they would love him to recreate the same high standards here in London. All David's questions were answered before he had even asked them.

"It's a very exciting project, but I would really like to give it a lot of thought before coming back to you with an answer. I'm very flattered that you've asked me to be part of it."

"Are you sure there's nothing else you want to ask us, David?"

"No, Marcus, You've covered everything in great detail."

"I nearly forgot to say that we know how much you love living in Saltmarsh Quay. We thought rather than you having to sell up and live in London full time, there would be a small apartment at the top of the hotel for you to use. That means on your days off you would be able to travel back to Norfolk."

That was the carrot being dangled in front of the stick. They knew there had to be a huge pull to get David to leave Norfolk and that it would never be just down to the wages. Back on the train, David's head was buzzing with excitement. He didn't need to give it any further thought. What a perfect life and work balance. Time off in his own cottage and the opportunity to lead one of the best five-star hotels in Europe. The one thing he did need was a cooling off period so he would not be giving them an answer for the next couple of weeks. However, he realised that this was the project to get him over his divorce. He could get things up and running, stay for ten years and then this would lead him nicely into retirement.

Chapter 8

The next morning David arrived at the hotel early. He had arranged a meeting with Glenda and Annie for the afternoon but had to be honest with them. Without saying that he was going to accept the job, he also needed to try and persuade Glenda to come with him. It would be the perfect opportunity for her to progress in the company and the hotel industry. There would be many things to discuss, but he was dreading telling the other members of staff that the hotel would be sold.

Just as he was walking through reception he noticed a woman coming down the main stairs, David thought that he recognised her, but couldn't put a name to her.

"Good morning, David. What's the weather doing today? Will I be able to get a nice long walk in? I thought I might venture down to the quay. How long do you think it will take me?"

"Oh, I'm so sorry, Miss Spring. I didn't recognise you."

"Well, David, that just shows I've done a good job of disguising myself. Must get on, so many beautiful places to discover. Have a lovely day."

David spent the rest of the morning going through emails. There was one from Marcus thanking him for coming up to London, telling him to give it as much time and thought as he needed.

But as with most things with Marcus there was a punch line and this one was not a good one. Word of mouth had spread that The Saltmarsh Cliff Hotel was going up for sale and they had been contacted by an agent representing an overseas buyer who was potentially interested in purchasing it as a holiday home. David took a deep breath. A 25-bedroom holiday home, not a hotel. Oh dear, if that's the case, his decision to take the London job was the right one.

Devel was on a mission. She was well wrapped up and the wig she had chosen really suited her complexion so there was no need to wear the hood. A little woolly hat would be sufficient. As she walked down the coastal path to the quay she could feel the cold breeze against her face, but it was a lovely experience and one she was not able to enjoy in California. She was just turning a little bend when a young couple came towards her. They greeted her with a 'hello' and mentioned how beautiful the view was. Devel was anonymous and felt excited. After about half an hour she arrived at the quay and was surprised to see how small and quaint it was. It looked just like an old postcard image. As she left the quay and headed up the street she saw a pub with signs saying 'Morning coffees, lunches, afternoon teas.' Dare she? Was she pushing her luck too far? This was dangerous.

"Good morning, madam. How I can help you? Coffee and biscuits or we do a very nice hot chocolate?"

"Hot chocolate would be perfect, thank you."

"If you would like to go and sit by the fire, I'll bring it over to you."

This was fun. Imagine being able to do this all the time while leading a normal life. Sadly she would stick out a mile back at home dressed like this. Devel had not really thought about home for a couple of days. Since venturing out with Annie it felt as if she was living two lives. The facelift had been successful, she could see a big difference, but as for feeling fresh and new that just seemed silly. Having drunk the chocolate and warmed herself by the fire, it was time to head back up the coastal path to the hotel.

Devel had always liked her own company, but the feeling she had taken from the day had been a special one. Perhaps when I get back to the States I should look for a home in a place just like this, she thought to herself. Oh, don't be silly, she continued. That doesn't exist, but you never know, it might.

David sat down with Glenda and Annie and told them all about the building and the company's plans to restore it to its original state but with all modern facilities. He tried not to sound too excited as both women expressed an interest. The whole meeting was very formal as no one wanted to show any emotion. David knew that Annie would not move to London, but Glenda was asking practical questions like how many staff would they require and what type of guest would they be attracting?

After the meeting David felt guilty for failing to mention the sale of The Saltmarsh Cliff Hotel. These were not just his employees, but also his friends and he should have been honest with them. For one thing, if potential buyers were coming to view the hotel they needed to know. David decided to sleep on it and then begin to prepare not just Annie and Glenda but all the staff for the months ahead.

Back at the hotel Devel poured herself a glass of wine and had a long soak in the bath. She had really enjoyed her day as the feeling of not having any pressure was lovely. She was also happy to avoid all the phone calls she normally would have received from acting colleagues full of news and gossip about films and television projects. Some days she had felt as though she were on a hamster wheel and not getting anywhere.

Things are going to change when I get back to the States. I've worked all my life, but now I'm going to start living my life just for me.

Chapter 9

A new day and one filled with practical jobs as David locked himself away in his office. First things first, he still had a hotel to run and they were just a couple of weeks away from Christmas Day. One good thing about this time of year was that he was not dealing with enquiries or trying to get business for the hotel. Everything was booked. The chef knew the catering requirements, housekeeping and reception were aware of the arrivals and departures. It was now just making sure that everyone was singing from the same hymn sheet. With all that having been organised, it was now time to put a plan together. David needed to speak to the company HR department about what he could and couldn't tell the staff, but first he needed to know the dates when potential buyers would be coming to view the hotel.

As the morning passed, he found himself thinking more and more about the London project. Owing to its location, David knew he could employ a top quality head chef and housekeeper, but he needed Glenda as a head receptionist. Glenda knew how David worked, but more importantly she would be his eyes and ears when he was not there. By the late afternoon he had received emails back answering most of his questions, but the most important reply requested him to call a staff meeting to inform everyone that the hotel was to be sold. He would also tell them that he had been offered a job, but had a few weeks to think about it.

Devel had also had a day of practicalities, dealing with emails and phone calls from America. Many of which were the usual type asking where she was, how she was missed at parties and asking when she was returning home. The more time she spent on all of this, she realised it would be far too late to do the one thing she really wanted to do – go for a walk. She had not heard from Max with any news of future auditions in the pipeline. She took that to mean that he wasn't looking for any more work for her since she had refused the audition for the toilet cleaning commercial.

It was starting to get dark, Devel had had enough for one day when another email appeared. She recognised it immediately as being from a top publisher as at least once a month they bombarded her with the same request, wishing to publish her autobiography. Normally she politely thanked them, but declined their offer. However, something in the back of her mind said 'Perhaps this is the time to say yes.' I've never written my life story, she thought to herself. There had been dozens of books written about her over the years, some good, some bad and many ugly ones without an ounce of truth in them. Perhaps now was the time to set the record straight, but one thing she was sure of was that if she decided to write her story, all the truth had to come out, failed marriages, the lot.

David had also had enough for one day. He felt as if he achieved a lot and it was time to go home and switch off. Devel felt the same, but she couldn't leave and it was far too late for a walk. Perhaps she could put on a disguise and take a taxi to a pub for a quiet meal.

David's phone rang...

"Hi, David, It's Devel. I'm sorry to bother you, but I need to find somewhere to go for a quiet meal, just a taxi ride away. Does the pub down on the quay serve meals in the evenings?"

"Hello, Devel. It does serve meals until nine o'clock. Oh, let me think. Not tonight. It's the one evening of the week the restaurant closes to give the chef a night off, but I'm sure we could find you a quiet table here in the hotel."

"I know, and the food here would be lovely, but I've been stuck in all day dealing with emails and paperwork. It's not really about the food. I just need to get out of these four walls."

"I really don't know what to suggest, but I know how you feel as my day has also been full of emails and phone calls and all I want to do is get out the office. I could drop you off somewhere as I'll be on my way home in a few minutes."

"I know this is not very professional, David, but would you like to join me for dinner somewhere? That's if you don't have any other plans."

"Oh, that would be lovely, but how about if I

cook for us at my cottage, then you won't have to..."

"I know what you mean. I won't have to dress up like an old bag woman."

"No, I was going to say that you won't have to have the worry of being recognised."

An hour later David found himself in his little kitchen making a Bolognese sauce to go with the pasta. Devel was sitting in his lounge, minus the wig, glasses and big coat, going through his CD collection. This felt very surreal. Here he was cooking for the one and only Devel Devonshire in his home. How stupid did that sound? With that he could hear the sound of Il Devo.

"Is my choice of music all right with you, David? I can remember seeing them years ago when they were the support act for Barbara Streisand. They've come such a long way since then."

David poured them both another glass of wine and continued with the cooking. Devel stood looking out to sea, the same landscape she had spent hours looking at over the last few weeks. It looked so different here down on the quay. She felt as if she was part of it rather than just a visitor taking it all in. She was smiling to herself about the size of the cottage. Never before had she been in a home so small, but the overwhelming atmosphere was homely, not just somewhere to live, and in a strange way she felt jealous.

By the time they had eaten and drunk a few more glasses of wine David had forgotten that

Devel was one of the top actresses in the world. They chatted about everything and it felt so normal. David hadn't planned on discussing his ex-wife as that was all in the past and he had moved on. He explained how happy they had been as a couple before moving to Norfolk when he was working in France and in London. She had worked and kept herself busy with different clubs and classes and the time they had spent together was good. However, arriving in Saltmarsh Quay she was bored. There were no shops or friends to meet for lunch and David was working all hours to get the hotel up and running. In a way he blamed himself for neglecting her. It was a case of someone else showing her the attention which he should have done.

Devel hadn't commented apart from saying that she was no advert for good relationships having been divorced. Although she talked about her life she did not go into any details about her marriages and David didn't enquire.

"David, you are so very lucky, living and working in such a beautiful part of the world. I'm so jealous. Saltmarsh Quay has a magic to it which I can't put my finger on, but it's perfect."

"Yes, I am, but look where you live, the Hollywood Hills! And what an exciting life you lead with millions of fans and all those fabulous films you've made. That's the perfect life."

"Sometimes, David, not everything you see is the truth. Yes, I'm an actress who lives in Hollywood, but that doesn't mean my life is perfect."

"I agree. Saltmarsh Quay is lovely and I will always live here, but it's going to be difficult leaving it to go to work."

"What? Are you leaving?"

"Oh dear, I've let the cat out the bag. You see, Devel, you're not the only one with a big secret. I suppose it won't hurt to tell you as everyone will know in a couple of days."

David went on to explain about the company buying the London hotel and selling The Saltmarsh Cliff Hotel.

"It's just what I need after the divorce, a new challenge. Something to spur me into action and get the brain ticking over."

"Yes, that's fine, but if you don't mind me saying, do you need spurring into action and a challenge? Why not settle for what you have?"

"Well, it's not quite as simple as that. If somebody bought the hotel and asked me to stay on as the manager, perhaps I would stay on, but sadly it looks like Saltmarsh Cliff might be bought for someone to use as a private home."

"What are you saying, David? I will never be able to come here again? The hotel will be gone?"

"Yes, I think that might be the case, but Devel, you have anywhere in the world to choose from. This is just a quiet little hotel in Norfolk. There must be far more stunning places to stay."

"No, David, you don't understand. Saltmarsh

Quay is magical. I could never find anywhere so perfect. It will be a disaster for the hotel and the quay. We've had such a lovely evening and to have it ending on such a sad note, I think it's time for me to go back to the hotel."

David waved Devel goodbye as she got into the taxi. Back in the cottage he could not understand how she took the news. It was so strange. The world was her oyster, so how could this little place cause her so much emotion? Perhaps it was the wine talking. He was baffled, but apart from that he had not enjoyed an evening so much for such a long time. He couldn't believe how much he talked about his past as he felt so comfortable with Devel. It was then he giggled to himself that here he was in his little two up two down, and he had just cooked dinner for one of the most famous women in the world. Time for bed, he thought.

Chapter 10

The next morning David was at the hotel very early as all the staff were due to come in for an afternoon meeting, during which he would explain the situation. He had no intention of worrying them about anything. It was a very profitable business which should sell quite quickly. As the morning progressed, he kept hearing Devel's comment.

"Do you need a challenge and spurring into action?"

The answer to that was simple. No, he didn't. His life was perfect, but he needed to earn money. He didn't need much, but it would be a few years before he could retire. Checking his emails, he saw one from Head Office informing him of the dates and times that potential buyers would be coming to look around. Everything was moving so fast. London was running at a million miles an hour! David needed to get out of the hotel for a couple of hours, clear his head and start thinking straight.

As he walked through reception a group of jolly ladies were coming in for a festive lunch. He felt bad that he wasn't there to personally greet them with the 'David' charm but Christmas and charm weren't his favourite things at that moment. Devel had put doubts in his head, but thinking about it, those doubts had been there all the time. He had been blocking them out.

Devel hadn't slept well. First of all, she felt bad about the way in which she had asked David whether he needed a new challenge. It was none of her business, but the main thing on her mind was why did this hotel mean so much to her? It was a magical place, but she had travelled all over the world and stayed at some of the most exclusive hotels in stunning locations. This felt different. This little hotel on the Norfolk cliffs had some sort of hold on her and she felt very strange about it. It wasn't excitement or nervousness, but something in her head told her that this was where she needed to be.

Glenda had discussed moving to London with her friends and family and had received differing reactions. Her friends were so excited, as they would be able to visit her in London and enjoy everything the big city had to offer. Her family looked at the practical side. Yes, it would be a fabulous career move, but did she really want to be living on the outskirts of London, catching the tube into work every day, moving from the peace and quiet of Norfolk to the bustling streets of London? What should she do?

The last thing in the world Annie wanted was not to be able to work at the hotel. The Saltmarsh Cliff Hotel had been her saving grace when Jim died, but she did not want to let this get her down. Financially, she didn't ask for much in life and perhaps this would be the time to start to wind down. Her philosophy in life was that everything happens for a reason.

It was cold but dry, the sort of day David enjoyed the most as there were no walkers or holiday makers on the path down to the little beach. This was another thing he would miss if he moved to London – being able to step out of the hotel into the peace and quiet. The tide was out, the sand and shingle looked so clean and untouched, any wind or breeze had disappeared and he was sheltered by the cliff. He wished he had brought a flask of coffee out with him. He remembered what Devel had said and she was right. This was a magical place. It was not just the stillness and the silence, it was special.

Devel had decided to walk down to the quay and have a sandwich in the pub. She was wrapped up warm in her disguise, and everything was starting to feel normal. In the time she had been going out, no one had even looked twice at her. Thankfully it was winter because it would be a completely different story in summer. As she turned to walk down the coastal path toward the quay, the wind increased its strength up and was blowing towards her. Devel was so disappointed as she really wanted to take her time and enjoy a few hours out of the hotel, but if she was honest with herself it was quite uncomfortable. Perhaps she should just walk around the grounds of the hotel, find a sheltered spot and sit and enjoy the view. If she walked in the opposite direction, the wind would be behind her so she started to head down the cliff path to the beach. She could see parts of the beach between the trees and the more she walked, the less the wind was blowing. She took her time and finally reached the bottom, so pleased that she had decided to change direction. A whole beach to herself, how fortunate she was. As she turned to find somewhere to sit and take in the view, she spotted someone else sitting on the big rock. Her morning had been spoilt as the last thing she wanted was to have a conversation with anyone. This could be the time her luck would run out and she would be recognised.

As she turned to walk to the other side of the beach she heard a familiar voice.

"Good morning. How are you today, Miss Spring?"

As she turned back she could see it was David. She left out a big sigh of relief and she felt her heart beating a little faster. 'Pull yourself together, Devel. You're a grown woman, not a teenager,' she said to herself.

"Hello, David. What brings you down here today?"

"I could ask you the same question, Devel, but I won't. I'm here thinking over a few things. You see, I said to someone that I needed a challenge and perhaps spurring into action, and they questioned it so that's got me thinking whether I do need that challenge."

"I'm so sorry, David. I was in no position to be

talking like that, but I couldn't understand how you would ever consider leaving this beautiful place."

"You're right, Devel. If the truth be known, I don't think I want to move. I don't need excitement, pressure or stress. There will be loads of that, but somehow I don't think I've got a choice."

Devel sat down beside David and for a few minutes neither of them spoke, until finally she looked him in the eyes and said:

"Why is this place so magical? I'm not really a spiritual person, David, but it makes me feel like a pin and Saltmarsh Quay is a magnet. I can't pull away from it, but most importantly, I don't want to."

It was another half an hour before either of them spoke another word. The silence was broken by the sound of David's phone ringing. He answered the call, but the conversation was short.

"Yes, that will be fine. Eleven o'clock tomorrow and I will arrange lunch for one-thirty. Are they aware that not all the suites will be available to view? Yes, we do have photos of all of them. Thank you."

After David ended the call he explained to Devel that three people acting on behalf of an overseas buyer were coming to look at the hotel. They had seen the website and had already discussed everything with one of the Directors. Devel didn't ask any questions and David didn't say anything else apart from the fact that he wasn't looking forward to telling all the staff later that afternoon. It was starting to get cold, so they decided to walk back up the hill to the hotel, chatting about Norfolk and the area as they did so. In fact, anything and everything, apart from themselves or the hotel. Once at the top, Devel wished David luck with the meeting and thanked him for a lovely morning.

It was gone nine o'clock before David returned home to his cottage. The meeting had been straight forward and he told all the staff the truth, even down to the fact that the company had offered him a job in London and that he was still contemplating whether or not to take it. He explained that people were coming to view the hotel the following day and that over the next few weeks he expected other hotel chains would also be coming to view it. He failed to mention, however, that The Saltmarsh Cliff Hotel might not remain a hotel as he didn't need to be dealing with any panic until the deal was completed. Since the end of the meeting at 4.30, nearly every member of staff had knocked on his door. They weren't concerned about the hotel having new owners, but they didn't want was a new boss. David felt drained. In all his years' managing hotels, this was different, so very different.

He poured a glass of wine and stood looking out onto the dark sea. The events of the next day didn't bother him. The Saltmarsh Cliff Hotel was not his property to sell. He was only there to show them around. He had carried out the duties he was employed for, opening a hotel for his employers and making it successful. He was very proud of his achievements, but this was not just any hotel. This was his life and his love. Every member of staff worked for him rather than for the company. They gave David so much time and respect, so how could he let it all go? He'd bounced back from his divorce, but not this. These people needed him, but more importantly, he needed them.

Chapter 11

The agents, two men and one woman, arrived promptly at eleven o'clock. They had coffee with David and were more than friendly. One of their main concerns was around security. How many gates were there around the perimeter, could anyone get from the beach to the hotel and did the coastal path lead into the hotel grounds? David answered the questions to the best of his ability before showing them around the hotel. Although they were only able to gain access to nine of the suites, they were satisfied with that. They were more interested in the public areas, how large a dining table could they fit into the restaurant? It needed to be big enough to cater for a minimum of 30 people. After measuring and placing dining chairs throughout the length and breadth of the room, it was estimated that the room could comfortably seat 44 people, and the kitchen and storerooms were more than adequate in size. After having been shown round the hotel, they asked David if he would join them for lunch to discuss a few more things. This was something he wasn't really happy about, but felt he had no option but to go along with their request.

Over lunch the agents were very forthcoming with information, although they didn't disclose any more about their client other than they spent a lot of time in this country and wanted to move out of London. Reading between the lines David detected that money wasn't an issue and the hotel was the first of dozens of potential properties they were viewing that came anywhere near the client's requirements. It was certainly the only one which the family could move into without doing any major refurbishments. However, that was not what David wanted to hear. He waved them off, understanding they would be back before Christmas, if not early January. Things were moving fast. There was only a week left before Christmas and David needed to keep all this from the staff. Anyway, a deal could be finalised in just a week as surveyors and solicitors needed to be involved. Back in his office, David phoned Marcus.

"Hi, David. Thank you so much. They were over the moon and could not praise you highly enough."

"So they've phoned you already? They can't even be at the end of the drive yet?"

"No, I had an email from them about an hour ago, asking us not to show the hotel to any other potential buyers."

"So what's going to happen now, Marcus?"

"I'll tell you, David. Have a fabulous Christmas there in Norfolk and get yourself ready for an exciting time here in London next year. I need to go. People to see. We'll speak again later in the week."

As he put the phone down David thought to

himself, "Christmas! How can this be a fabulous Christmas when the staff will lose their jobs and I have to take a job I don't really want? This certainly wasn't the Christmas he had planned.

David wasn't the only one having a bad day. Devel had been stuck in her suite all day as it was windy and cold, so there was no prospect of her taking a walk. She spent the morning dealing with emails from her friends, who again were enquiring as to her whereabouts and her plans for Christmas. She also had been looking in the mirror and noticed that the swelling on her face had gone down. With just a similar coloured foundation, no one would tell that she'd had a facelift, which was rather ironic really as the object of the exercise was to look different. Or was it? Should she fly back to the States for Christmas? Did she really want to spend her time going to parties? She hated talking trivia to people she didn't really care for, but if it rained here in Norfolk, she would be stuck in these rooms. Why, oh why, had she put herself through all of this? She had seen the agents getting into a car and driving off and wondered how things had gone? Poor David. Just as he had sorted out his life and was in a good place, it was all being taken away from him. She did feel sorry for him. 'Snap out of it, Devel,' she said to herself. 'You're the one who got yourself into this. Get yourself out of it.' She picked up the phone and it was answered immediately:

"Hello, David Rose, speaking. How I can help

you?"

"David, if your day's been anything like mine, you'll need cheering up and what better way than a few glasses of wine, a beautiful meal cooked by an American and a chat? It's a bit presumptuous really as I'm inviting myself to cook for you in your own home. You can say no, but you wouldn't want one of your guests to be unhappy with her stay, would you?"

"Well, Devel, if you put it like that how can I say no? Just let me know the ingredients you need and the time you'll be coming, and I will get it sorted."

David was standing under the shower thinking how mad this situation was. Here he was in his own home, getting ready to sit down to dinner with Devel Devonshire, and the world famous actress had cooked it for him. It was completely insane. Devel had poured herself a glass of wine, put on a Gladys Knight CD and was preparing the fish for her paella. She felt quite at home, but more importantly, all the day's frustrations had passed. Any thoughts of going home for Christmas had well and truly vanished.

"Something smells good."

"Yes, it's getting there, but the secret to my paella is not to rush it. I've poured you a glass of red. Is that okay."

"Perfect, thank you. Just what I need after today's visit."

"David, you don't have to talk about. It's

personal and between you and the staff. I don't need to know."

David needed to talk to someone about it. He wasn't seeking advice but as dinner would be another half an hour, he went over the day's events. Devel mentioned how sad it would be for Saltmarsh Quay to lose its biggest employer as many families relied on the hotel for a living, not just directly, but its closure would impact on other businesses, from the pubs to gift shops to taxis. David hadn't fully appreciated that if a buyer was going to be using it as a home rather than a hotel, it would be the beginning of the end for Saltmarsh Quay.

The meal was perfect as Devel was a good cook. Over dinner they talked mostly about food and restaurants around the world. David laughed so much when Devel mentioned the places where she had eaten and the chefs who had tried to impress her but it had turned out to be a disaster. She could not recall the amount of times she had left events and restaurants, gone back to a hotel and had to order room service, but that was all part of being famous. They finished dinner, loaded the dishwasher and sat down by the fire with another glass of wine.

Outside it was wet and windy, but the cottage with its crackling fire was so cosy and they both felt relaxed.

"You're miles away, staring into the fire, Devel. What do you see in there?"

"Sorry. I'm not ignoring you, but I am miles away. Yes, hundreds of miles away. You've been very open and honest with me about your personal life, David, and more so your feelings. However, all you know about me is that I'm an actress hiding in your beautiful hotel while she recovers from a facelift. I wouldn't blame you as I'd do the same, but you've probably investigated me on the Internet. It's full of photos of me out and about in America, but you won't find anything about any acting projects I've done in the last few years. Hence the facelift. I need to work, but not for the money. It's all I've ever known. I'm bored and restless at home, but here in England it's as if I've stepped off a merry-go-round and it feels good."

David topped up their glasses and Devel started to tell him about her life. She had been fortunate as her parents weren't pushy show business people. In fact, when she was 14 a major awarding winning film wanted Devel to take on a part. She had turned it down as she wanted to spend the summer with her family. She wasn't jealous or sad about the actress who was later given the role having won the awards, as she was just happy to have spent the holidays with the people she cared about most. Once she was old enough to make decisions for herself and take control of her career, that's when she really came into her own. Everything was negotiated between Devel and her agent and everything was planned years in advance. That's when she hit the big time.

Her career was perfect with job after job, the money was rolling in and Devel was travelling the world. That was how it was for a good 30 years. They were very happy times as producers and directors said they loved working with her, not just because she was a fine actress but because she wasn't a diva. She was always on time and well-rehearsed, which made their lives easier. Devel loved meeting new people and working with fresh new talent and she was never, ever jealous of younger actresses coming through the ranks. The problem now was that there weren't any jobs available for women of her age. Devel went on to tell David how her agent was dropping her and prior to arriving in England she felt her life was over. However, over the last few weeks she felt she had accepted that her acting days could be over.

"That's the highs, but David, there were lows. I think the collective name for them is ex husbands."

"Keep to the good stuff, Devel. I don't need to know the bad things."

But Devel was on a roll and she wanted to talk about it. She explained that her first husband was an actor on a film with her, filming together every day for three months and having to appear at events, promoting the film. It had been wonderful. They were both young, had fallen madly in love and got married within weeks of meeting each other. Once the filming and publicity was over it was on to the next job for both of them. Neither were to blame, but they just grew apart and that was the end of her first marriage.

The next one was quite a few years later. He was the brother of a mutual friend and they had known each other for about 10 years. When Devel needed a date for a premiere or an event, he would step in to be her partner. Devel didn't really know how it had happened, but they ended up getting married. However, after a few years they too drifted apart. He was the only ex husband that Devel was still on speaking terms with and they sometimes still holidayed together, but that was the end of her second marriage.

Her third marriage was a completely different situation. Drake was a Texas business man, tall, dark handsome and very rich. Not that that bothered Devel as she was wealthy in her own right. Drake was besotted with her and worshipped the ground she walked on. As she had two failed marriages behind her, there was no way she wanted to rush into a third. It took Drake over two years to persuade Devel to marry him. He would fly all over the world to be with her, he was so attentive and they had such good times together. Sadly she wasn't the only one he was attentive with and the American press had photos of a string of younger woman who Drake was seeing. That was the end of marriage three.

Moving on to marriage number four, Clifford

was lovely, He was slightly older than her and was happy to let Devel do her own thing while he went off to play golf. When she wasn't working they would go away on holiday. Clifford never once had a problem with Devel being recognised and when fans wanted a photo or an autograph he would just stand back until they had finished. Eight years ago they had rented a house for Christmas near to Clifford's family in Nashville as both his son and his daughter from his first marriage lived there. His son, Keith, was a music producer. There were about 12 for the Christmas celebration and it was such a beautiful time as they were all so happy. That Christmas was so special. Recalling this past event, Devel started to get teary and a little emotional.

"Look. This is personal, Devel. You don't need to talk about it."

"David, I want to. I don't generally talk about it and I should, but you don't know what I'm talking about. You won't have read this on the Internet."

"Why should I? You're a guest in our hotel. What's happened in your past is no interest to us. It's what happens at the hotel that concerns me."

She went on to tell David that on the morning of New Year's Eve, Clifford and Keith went to the grocery store, but on their way back a lorry swerved from one side of the road and went straight into them. They were both killed instantly. By the time Devel had finished telling David, she was in a terrible state. David sat beside her and tried his best to comfort her. It was a long time before she calmed down and she explained that this was the first time she had cried and talked about their deaths for seven years.

"I moved on. That's what I've always done. That's what I've learnt from my work. When a film ends, move on to the next. When I've been in a TV series, perhaps for a couple of years, I walked out the door when the filming was finished and that was that, on to the next job. In my profession there's no time for nostalgia. You have to keep moving."

"But, Devel, your husband died. You need to grieve. Throwing yourself into something will help, but at some point you really do have to let go and grieve for the love you have lost."

David's arms around her made her feel secure. That was something she hadn't felt for a long while and the thought of leaving Saltmarsh Quay and the magical feelings that came with it, now scared her.

"Do you mind if I stay here tonight? Do you have a blanket? I can sleep on the sofa."

"Don't be silly. I'll show you to the spare room. Is there anything else you need?"

"No, just a good night's sleep. I'm drained. That's something I should have done years ago, but I've never met anyone with whom it felt right to share these things with. Oh, David. You're a kind, generous man who has shown me that life should be slowed down and that it's important to enjoy what's happening now and not run head first into the future."

As David showed her to the room, she turned and looked into his eyes and kissed him. They both stood there not knowing what to do, but they both realised that this was the time to say good night.

Chapter 12

David was up early and had crept out of the cottage, not wanting to wake Devel. He scribbled a note telling her to make herself at home and stay as long as she wanted, and also thanked her for a lovely evening. Once at the hotel, he got stuck into the final Christmas preparations and put any thoughts of the hotel closing to the back of his mind.

Devel had been awake for hours. Once she heard David leave for work, she was up, making herself a coffee. She smiled when she read David's note. Even though it had been a very emotional evening, he was right. It has been lovely. Devel appreciated the offer to stay in the cottage, but she was eager to get back to the hotel. It had stopped raining and the wind had died down, so the walk to The Saltmarsh Cliff Hotel would be the perfect start to the day.

***

There was a knock on the door of David's office.

"Come in. Oh, hello, Annie. How are you today?"

"I'm fine thanks, but I've just taken Miss Spring's breakfast tray up and she's not in her room. I'm a bit concerned."

"She's probably gone for an early walk as it's not raining."

"Yes, but her bed hasn't been slept in."

"Oh, I don't think we need worry, Annie. Give it

an hour or so and check again. While you're here, is everything ready for the Christmas break? Is there plenty of linen? I don't know why I've asked you that, as you're the most organised member of staff. I'm sorry."

"Thank you. Like I've said before, I only do what you employ me to do. By the way, can I ask you something? I won't be offended if you can't give me an answer, but the people who were looking around the hotel yesterday, which hotel chain are they from?"

"I will answer you, Annie, as I know it won't go any further. They're not from a hotel company. They're agents for a private buyer who wants to buy the hotel to use as a home."

"Oh dear. That was what I feared. Does anyone else know about this?"

"No, just you and me, and I'd like to keep it that way until the Christmas celebrations are over if that's all right. Sorry, Annie, but someone else does know. I mentioned it to Devel. It's a long story, but I know she won't say a word."

Devel had a lovely walk back to the hotel. She had missed her walk the previous day and this made it even more special. Once back at the hotel, she showered and switched her laptop on. There were hundreds of emails. The first one she read was from Max. Whether he was still her agent, she didn't really know.

"Hi, Devel, where are you? Contact me

straightaway, but first read this from a Los Angeles newspaper."

Does anyone know the whereabouts of actress Devel Devonshire who has not been seen at her Hollywood home for over a month? Her agent has confirmed that she isn't working on any projects at the moment. We will pay a significant amount of money for information and photographs.

Every email from friends and acquaintances was the same. If Devel had seen these a few days ago it would have upset her, but after the evening with David talking about her past and the tragedy with Clifford, she just laughed. "Oh, my God. All the terrible things that are going on in the world and this paper wants a photo of me. Perhaps I should take one and claim the money." She deleted the emails and then made a call to Frederick, her lawyer in America. Of course, he knew where she was and wasn't a bit concerned, but started the conversation off by saying that he was going to claim the money.

Devel spent an hour on the phone having a conversation she should have done seven years previously. It hadn't been for the lack of trying on Frederick's part as he had continually nagged her, but hadn't got anywhere with it. Today, for the first time, she talked and listened about things concerning Clifford's will and finances as today the time had been right. Despite being so tired and drained, in a strange way she felt alive, free and content. There was a knock on the door. Annie had come to see if she needed anything. Devel appreciated Annie's discretion as there was no mention of her not sleeping at the hotel.

"Actually, Annie, there is something. What are you doing this evening? Would you like to have dinner with me here in the room? I think you'll be able to help me with a few things?"

"That would be very nice, thanks."

That was sorted but what was she going to do about this stupid newspaper thing? She'd have to do something before someone here in Norfolk tried to claim the money. After an hour or so staring out to sea and drinking lots of coffee, she came up with an answer. Malcolm, one of the drivers she had hired in the States for years had a son, Steven, who was a journalist here in the UK. She'd known him ever since he was a young boy and perhaps he could help. She searched him out on the Internet and found out that he was working for one of the English broadsheets. Perfect. She sent Malcolm a text asking for his son's mobile number and in response received a lovely text asking her if she was all right and whether she needed help with anything as he could drop everything if need be. She texted back thanking him, and saying how stupid all this newspaper thing was and joked how she was going to claim it for herself.

Devel immediately managed to get through to Steven. He was aware of the story, but did say that he'd found it funny. Between the two of them, they came up with a plan that would benefit them both. He'd get credit from his editor for getting an exclusive, and she would get the newspaper off her back. A few white lies may have to be told along the way, but whoever said everything in the press was the truth?

David received a phone call from Marcus telling him the potential buyer wouldn't be coming to see the hotel until the New Year as he was off to one of his homes in the sunshine for Christmas, and the company would wait until after his visit before they let anyone else view it. That was good news, so he could just get on with running the hotel.

Devel had a busy afternoon dealing with emails to Frederick and her accountant, Samuel. She knew it should have been done years ago, but there was no need to start thinking like that. The one thing she didn't know was exactly how wealthy Clifford was. When she'd met him, she had been aware that he'd sold two successful companies and made a lot of money from them, but since money was never an issue with either of them, it wasn't discussed. The only thing she did know was that if anything happened to Clifford, his estate would be divided three ways between his son, daughter and herself and as far as she knew that's what had happened. As Clifford's son died in the accident, this money went to his wife and children. Devel didn't know how much money she had inherited as every time

Samuel tried to talk to her about money, she always told him that was what he was employed to do...

"I'm the actress and I earn the money. You're the accountant and you invest the money. I promise not to do any investments as long as you promise not to act."

To say Samuel's explanation of how Clifford was an astute business man, having sold both the companies at the right time to buy a small island was a shock to Devel, would be an understatement. She had known for years that she would never have to work again, as she was a very wealthy actress but now with Clifford's money this took her into another league. Samuel told her she was in a position to start her own film company, which was something he knew she had considered many years previously. She thought that would have been good. She'd never have to audition again. There was so much to think about and plan, but what she was really looking forward to was having dinner with Annie. There was so much she wanted to ask her about Saltmarsh Quay, the hotel and David. Yes, she wanted to find out more about this caring and thoughtful, hotel manager.

David and Glenda had spent the afternoon going over the Christmas guest list. Every room was booked. More than three quarters of the guests had stayed there before and the hotel staff knew all their likes and dislikes. Hopefully, the other guests would settle in well. Glenda had asked David if he had made a decision on the future and he had been honest with her. If a new company took over, there may not be a job for him, so he would probably have to accept the London job offer, but very reluctantly. Glenda felt the same. Yes, it would be the perfect career move, but did she really want that? Glenda pointed out to David that the company had put a block on the computer for taking any bookings after 1st March. Why did he think that had happened?

"I don't know, but I will email Marcus."

"But surely a new company would want to take over a fully booked hotel. It's all very strange."

It was 7.30 before David left to go home. He was feeling slightly deflated, but it was a question of painting a false smile for the next couple of weeks just to get through Christmas and the New Year's Eve ball. He could then put out a few feelers around Norfolk. As he walked to his car, he saw Annie coming in.

"You look very nice, Annie. Are you off somewhere?"

"Yes, I'm having dinner with Miss Spring. Apparently, she wants to pick my brains. I'm looking forward to this as she's been different for the last few days. I don't know why, but she seems happier."

"Well, have a good time and I'll see you tomorrow."

"Good night, David. Please don't worry. I'm sure

everything will turn out for the best."

The chef had cooked Devel and Annie a lovely chicken stew followed by apple crumble and custard, traditional hearty winter food. Devel told Annie all about the newspaper story and her plans to stop it from getting out of hand. She needed Annie to help prepare the suite the next day as Steven was coming in the afternoon and she also wanted Annie to order some flowers. Steven was bringing a friend who would do Devel's hair ready for a photograph as evidence that she was still alive.

"Now Annie, tell me what's going on down on the quay. I just love it so much. Do they have any special celebrations or traditions at Christmas? David tells me the hotel is full for Christmas and the atmosphere is really lovely."

"Yes, the quay is lovely. A lot of the cottages are second homes for people from London and they all come up for the Christmas period. It does become quite busy, but in a lovely way. As for the hotel, it's going to be very emotional as it's our last year here all together. David mentioned that you were aware of the situation and it's going to so devastating for Saltmarsh Quay as so many people rely on this hotel for an income. The other businesses need the hotel guests to spend money. No one's going to gain if these people buy the hotel. It's going to be terrible."

"But, Annie, it's not happened yet, and until it's signed on the dotted line they don't own it. You have to be positive. It might not happen."

Devel quickly changed the subject and asked Annie to help her choose something to wear for her photo and to decide on where would the best place to have it taken. They selected a very pale blue Chanel suit with a string of pearls and decided that Devel should sit on the sofa with the paintings behind her. She had no intention of having the sea behind her. She might have been forced into giving an interview, but she certainly wasn't going to let anyone know what part of Great Britain she was in.

"Thank you so much for your help. Why don't we have another glass of wine and sit here looking out to sea. I never tire of this view. I know hours can pass and it's just a mass of sea, but there's something very magical about it."

"I know. I never get tired of it either. That's why whatever happens with the hotel, I will never move away. This is my home forever."

"What do you think David will do? I get the impression he doesn't really want the job in London. Do you know, Annie, over the few weeks I've been here, I've become very fond of him, but that I've also come to love everything about Saltmarsh Quay. It really does have a special magic about it."

"Yes, it is magical. We're like a family at the hotel, but families move on. Times and people change, Devel, it's a fact of life. Whatever David decides to do will be right for him. I only hope his life doesn't just become all work. I would love nothing more for him than to find happiness in his personal life. If there's anyone in the world who deserves it, it's him. I think it's about time I was heading home. You have a very busy day tomorrow. What time would you like me here?"

"It will be a very relaxed day, Annie. Steven will chat to me while his friends make me look good. We will have a spot of lunch here in the suite and hopefully the interview will be published a few days later. That will stop all the silly fuss about where is Devel Devonshire? Only the lounge will need a quick tidy, so you don't need to be here any earlier than normal."

"Okay, and thank you so much for a lovely evening. I've really enjoyed myself, I still can't believe here I am with one of the most famous women in the world. I enjoy your company so much, Devel."

"Likewise, Annie, and please don't worry about the hotel. I get the feeling something good will happen, and like I said, until things are signed and sealed it's still The Saltmarsh Cliff Hotel and not a private home. Good night, and I'll see you in the morning."

Chapter 13

Devel was up early as she had so much on her mind. First and foremost, she needed to get this silly interview over with. Over the years she had given thousands of interviews but the vast majority of them had been scripted as that's what the film companies had demanded. There was always a list of subjects which could be asked, and an even longer one of topics which couldn't be discussed. This interview would not be any different. She had written notes, a back story of why she was in the UK and what she had been up to in the last few weeks. Devel laughed to herself, 'Oh, I forgot to mention the facelift. What a shame that might get left out of the interview.'

Annie gave the suite a clean and laid a table with drinks and snacks. Devel washed her hair ready for the hairdresser to work some magic.

"Hello, Steven. It's so lovely to see you. It's been far too long. More importantly, a huge thank you for putting yourself out at such short notice."

"No, Devel, thank you for giving me this exclusive interview. Can I introduce you to Kim?"

"Very nice to meet you, Kim. I really hope you can do something with this mop of hair. I've not really been looking after it while I've been here in Norfolk. The sea air has dried it up."

"I'm sure that won't be a problem."

"Now both of you, please help yourself to some refreshments."

Chit chat over, Annie sat at the back of the room just in case Devel needed anything. Her hair styling was progressing well, and everything was quite jolly. It was time for Devel to take control and put her plan into action. She did feel slightly guilty about having to tell a few small white – well, actually large black lies, but this was a scoop for Steven and as it would help his career it was a bit of a win for both of them.

"So, Steven, as you can imagine, over all the years I've given thousands of interviews and they've always been a little boring. Same old questions. What am I working on? Who's my favourite leading man? What hobbies do I have? The list just goes on and on, so this time I thought I'd do something a little different. I hope you don't mind. What I'd like to do is chat to you about what I've been up to and then you can add the question afterwards, if that's all right."

Steven was more than happy with this. He had no intention of tricking Devel as she had been very good and generous to both him and his family for many years.

"That will be perfect and before anything is printed, Devel, you're more than welcome to change anything."

So Devel sat back and was ready to go. Kim only needed to do a few touches before the photos were taken, so she decided to go out for a walk while they chatted. Steven was ready with his Dictaphone and Devel hit the ground running, "I hadn't really planned on staying in the UK as long as I have. The reason I came in the first place was to have a meeting with a new British production company about a part they wanted me to play. Sadly it didn't work for either them or myself. I just wasn't right for the part. I had a few days spare before I was to fly back to the States and I decided to see a couple of theatre shows. I hate the fuss that accompanies me when I turn up at shows, so I bought a couple of wigs and glasses and off I went. No one recognised me. It was lovely just being normal, but you see, Steven, it has become an obsession, the theatre not the wigs! I have now seen nearly every play and musical here in the West End. I've also been to art galleries and museums. There's so much happening here in London, I just love it. You won't believe it, but I've had to change my flights so many times and now I've decided to stay here in London until the New Year as I'm enjoying it so much. As for the future, there's a very important project I'm looking into. It involves me, but not in an acting role. I really wish I could talk about it, but my lawyers have forbidden me to. I'm so sorry, Steven, but hopefully all will be revealed in the New Year."

The whole thing was completely untrue, but Devel needed to be left alone and hopefully this would put a stop to all the questioning. Steven was really happy with the story and did ask the one question that she couldn't answer honestly, which was her favourite London performance?

"Oh, Steven. I've seen so many that it would be very unfair for me to answer that. I've loved so many of them and theatre work is so strenuous. Eight shows a week and before you ask, I can give you another exclusive. Devel Devonshire will not be trending the boards now or at any time in the future."

She went on to say that Christmas was going to be spent with friends in the UK. She loved all the British traditions and come the New Year, fingers crossed, she was very excited to be getting involved in her new project.

Annie spent the whole time giggling to herself. What an actress! She was starting to believe the story herself. She knew Steven didn't believe a word of it, but he had a story and he was happy. Kim came back and finished the hair, Devel did her own make-up and the setting was perfect, not too bright. It could have been any five star hotel in London. No one would ever guess Devel had a facelift. The whole morning had been, as they say in the theatre, smoke and mirrors.

"Steven, it's been so nice to see you and I can't thank you enough for doing this for me. It was so kind, and Kim you made me look so good in the photos. Steven, please make sure Kim gets a mention in the article as I think she should be credited for not just the hair, but the styling as well."

"But, Devel, I only did your hair. You did everything else."

"No, I insist, Kim. You made the whole process so enjoyable."

"Thank you, Devel. I'm so grateful. It will really do my career the world of good. I cannot thank you enough."

"It's my pleasure. Both of you have made an aging actress feel very special today. Have a safe journey home and by the way, as a little thank you I've booked a table for two at the Ritz for tomorrow night for you both, just a little something for my appreciation."

They could not thank Devel enough. They left the hotel, job completed, just as Devel had planned. Hopefully, that would be the end of this stupid 'where is Devel Devonshire' thing. Once she had got changed, removed all the makeup and Annie tidied around, they sat down with a glass of wine, looked at each other and laughed.

"It's all one big game, Annie, everything. It's not just the acting and newspaper industry. Life is just one big game."

When Annie got home that night she sat there for a moment and reflected on how the last few weeks had changed. Here was this world famous actress who came to the hotel a little nervous, worried and very vulnerable, but now was so different. Confident was the word Annie would use, but there was something else. How could Devel be so certain that everything with the hotel would work out well? What did she know that David didn't?

Devel loved having the Internet at the touch of a button in front of her. Christmas Day was only five days away and she needed presents for people. Not just the normal every day kind of present, but things that she needed to give some thought to. All of the hotel staff had been so kind and caring and she wanted to thank them. What better way to do that than on Christmas Day?

David had a day off from the hotel. He too was thinking of presents for staff and he had also made a few phone calls about potential jobs in Norfolk as he had decided that London wasn't for him. He worked out how much money he needed to live on and was feeling very positive. He knew the hotel would not exist in a few months' time, but planned to make the last Christmas at The Saltmarsh Cliff Hotel a very special one for him, the guests and more importantly, the staff. One they would never forget.

Chapter 14

Christmas Day was only a couple of days away, the hotel was quiet as all the conferences and Christmas lunches and dinners had finished. It was just a question of getting ready for the guests who were arriving to celebrate over the Christmas period. Devel had been busy wrapping presents for the staff and spending a lot of time on the phone to America. Most importantly, today her interview would be published. David and Glenda were organised and it was all rather like the calm before the storm.

Annie took the newspaper up to Devel as soon as it arrived. The two of them spread it out on the table and read it. Steven had done a brilliant job, the photo was perfect and everything Devel wanted to get across was correct. There was no clue as to where she really was and what she had been doing. She phoned Steven to thank him and he was so pleased to have been able to help.

"At least that's over and done with, Annie. I can now can get on with enjoying myself. First of all I might just email the article to the newspaper in the States and ask for the reward money. Oh, Annie, there was something I wanted to ask you. I was wondering whether any of the other staff have figured out who I am yet? I'm beginning to feel a little guilty as the weeks go on because everyone has been so nice to me."

"No, Devel. I've not heard one person mention your name. That's not to say there hasn't been a lot of rumours going around, which has been quite funny."

"So not even Glenda knows? I speak to her on the phone at least once a day."

"No, not at all."

"Annie, do you think it would be all right to tell her?"

"That's up to you, Devel, if you think that's wise."

"Yes, I do. If she is free sometime today, could you ask her to call in and see me?"

David thought he was in for a nice relaxing day until he got an urgent call from Marcus telling him that he was on his way. That was the last thing David wanted. Perhaps it was to tell him that perspective buyers had pulled out.

Annie explained everything to Glenda, who was quite shocked. She didn't have a clue and was very excited to be going to meet Devel. In the meantime she was slightly on edge because of Marcus' visit. She had taken the initial phone call for David, who was certainly not a happy man today, which was so out of character for him.

"Hello, Glenda. Is David in his office? Could you get some strong coffee sent in, please?"

"Okay, Marcus, and yes, David is expecting you."

You could have cut the atmosphere with a knife, but David was having none of it. The company needed him more than he needed the job. He was completely sure the information he was being accused of leaking hadn't come from Norfolk.

"Marcus, there are only two people in the hotel who are aware of the potential buyers and that's myself and Annie. I've not told anybody and Annie would not breathe a word of it to anyone. Perhaps one of the people dealing with it in London has said something or the prospective buyer may have said something. Anyway, how has all this come about? Surely they're going to buy it and that's that. The company must be happy as they have a buyer."

Marcus went on to explain what had actually happened. Two days ago the company received an email enquiring about the sale of the hotel and how much it was up for sale for. They politely replied that it was not up for sale but thanked them for their interest. Another email arrived saying they were interested in purchasing it and they would be keeping it as a hotel and not a private home. The final sentence was: 'surely it's in the company's interest to sell it as a business as the staff would still have jobs. The publicity that the company would get for staff losing jobs, wouldn't look good.'

"We don't need publicity like this, David. We are a caring business. We treat out staff well, as you know."

"Perhaps, Marcus, they have a point. What do you know about them?"

"Nothing apart from they're an American

company."

That was the word: 'American'. David felt sick. Of course, he and Annie weren't the only people who knew. He'd told Devel, but surely she would not have mentioned it to anyone. What did she have to gain from it?

"Are you, all right, David? You've gone quiet."

"I don't think we need this a couple of days before Christmas."

To make matters worse, Marcus was full of apologies for accusing David. Of all the people in the company, David would have been the last person to blame. As Marcus left he knew he needed to speak to Devel about this. He phoned her room, but did not receive an answer. She had probably gone for a walk. It would have to wait.

The wig and dark glasses were getting on Devel's nerves. How she longed not to have to wear them, but after spending so much time and effort convincing people that she was in London, the last thing she needed was to be discovered in Norfolk. As she started to make her way down to the little beach, she felt very pleased with the article. Once an actress always an actress!

David knew where Devel would be and apart from the problem he had, he was looking forward to seeing her. Just half an hour in her company would make his day, but should he spoil it by mentioning the strange emails? As he walked to the coastal path, he could smell Devel's perfume. His stomach turned. Whether it was nerves or excitement, he wasn't really sure.

"Good morning, David. Are you following me? We seem to have something in common. We both love this little beach."

"I know. I just wish I could get down here more often. It's so sheltered. A lot of people don't realise that. If they did, I think it would be full. It's the perfect place to think things through."

"Have you still not decided what you're going to do when the hotel's sold?"

"I've decided on one thing. I'm not going to London to work. I'm staying here in Norfolk, doing what I don't know yet, but the bright lights of the city don't have any attraction for me. The company don't know that yet, they've got other things on their minds."

This was David's opportunity to talk about it without asking whether Devel had mentioned it to anyone. Her manner didn't give anything away, but then she was an actress after all.

"Well, David, they do have a point. A lot of people and businesses will suffer. Perhaps they would be better to sell it as a running hotel and before you ask, David, I haven't sent them an email."

"Oh, Devel I didn't think you would. Now stop all this hotel talk and tell me about your interview. I've read it today and it's really good. Annie told me what a fun morning you had with the journalist."

By the time they had chatted about everything and anything two hours had flown by. They both loved being down on the beach, but more than that they loved being in each other's company. As they walked back up the costal path and turned into the hotel grounds they could hear a lorry coming down the drive. When it came into view, they saw 'American News' written on the side.

"David, it's one of two things. Either someone's found out about the sale of the hotel or someone's aware of that strange actress in the hotel."

"This is private property. I'll get rid of them. If you walk around the back of the trees and go in the side entrance, I'll let you know what it's all about?"

David managed to get rid of them, but Devel had been right. Someone from where she had ordered Christmas presents had put two and two together and when she had paid on her credit card and contacted the newspaper which was looking for her, that was their way of getting back at Devel, to let the news crew know she had been found out. It was bound to happen at some point and David thought it was better now than when she first arrived with bandages. After he had told Devel all of this, her reaction was that as bad weather was forecasted over Christmas, she wouldn't be going out walking. "I'll be in my suite, so let them have a sad few days in their lorry out on the main road," she explained. The thing was, to put them off the scent, a plan had to be executed.

Chapter 15

The TV crew didn't stay long once they realised they couldn't get into the hotel and with Christmas a few days away, they wanted to go home to their families for festive celebrations. Devel wasn't really bothered as there was no way they'd get a photo of her. The weather was very wet and windy, so she wouldn't be able to go out for a walk, but that was fine as she had lots to be getting on with. She had decided to tell close friends she was spending Christmas in England. She had received text and emails from people about her interview but not one of them had made any comment on how she looked. In one way it was good that no one had guessed about the facelift, but on the other hand if she didn't look any different, had it all been a waste of time? Another decision which had seemed such a big issue for the last few weeks was her disguise. The hiding was now over, from now on she was going to be Devel.

The meeting she had with Glenda the previous day had helped her in several ways. Glenda had explained that the success of the hotel was down to one thing, David, his management skills and the way he treated and worked with his staff. Devel wanted to know more about David's ex-wife. Whereas she knew not to ask Annie, as she wasn't a gossip, Glenda was a little freer with information.

From all accounts, whenever she came to the hotel she looked down on the staff and walked around as if she owned the place.

Devel had made another decision and needed Glenda's help. She wanted to know whether it was possible for her to go down into the restaurant for Christmas Day lunch. Glenda had said it would as she wanted to surprise David.

David's day was not going well. Marcus had been on the phone again. This time he wasn't angry about where the news about the hotel sale had come from. He explained that the Board of Directors had held an emergency meeting as they needed to limit any publicity about the sale. The American interest was very serious and they were now in talks with them. Marcus told him that they had also been in contact with the agents for the foreign businessman and explained that he could face a backlash as so many people would lose their jobs and business would suffer if he moved to Saltmarsh Quay. Marcus warned him that he probably wouldn't receive a very friendly welcome.

"David, there's just one thing bothering me. It's how we've never heard of this American company before. They have no other hotel interests as all their business is connected to the film industry. I can't put my finger on how up to date they are with everything at the hotel and Saltmarsh Quay. It's a real mystery."

"Well, Marcus, as you know, we do have guests

from all over the world. Anyone could be feeding the information."

After ending the phone call, David knew he had to speak to Devel. If she was buying the hotel, it would be lovely for all the staff as they would still have their jobs, but where did he fit into her plans? At the moment he was far too busy for that as the Christmas guests had arrived. The next day he needed to discuss the final preparations with Glenda and the head chef. These guests were paying thousands of pounds to stay in the hotel for the Christmas period, so everything had to be perfect. There was a knock at his door.

"Come in. Oh, hello, Annie. How's everything going? Stupid question, sorry. If anyone's ready for all the arrivals it's you. What can I do for you?"

"I've been asked to deliver a note to you. Everything in housekeeping is sorted, I'm on top of it all and Devel doesn't need anything for the rest of the day. She says she will be busy all day and doesn't want to be disturbed. If you need any help with things, just give me a shout."

"Thanks, Annie, you're a star. Where would I be without you?!"

David opened the handwritten note and read the contents:

Dearest David

I would like to invite you to join me for dinner in my suite on Christmas Eve at around 8.30. I'm aware that it's a very busy time for you, but Glenda informs me that after you've greeted the guests for pre-dinner drinks you will be off duty until Christmas Day morning. I've arranged with the chef for dinner to be served at 9.00. I'm very much looking forward to seeing you.

Devel

David felt his stomach flutter. There was nothing more he wanted to do than spend time with Devel, but how could he ask her why she was buying the hotel. Annie had made it quite clear that she wasn't to be disturbed, but perhaps she had invited him so she could talk about the sale. There were so many questions.

Devel was in full swing as more parcels had arrived. However, they could wait until later as first of all she had a very important phone call to make. It was still very early in the States, but as her solicitor was making a press release at 10.00, she thought she had better get it over with.

"Good morning. It's Devel Devonshire. Could put me through to Max, please?"

"Hello, Devel. I've been emailing you as I've been desperate to speak to you since I read your interview in the British press. You really should have passed it through me first, but no harm done. Actually, darling, it's gone mad here in the office and it's done you a lot of good. I've had more enquiries for you in one day than I've had in months. I think we're onto a winner. You do need to be back in the States by the fourth of January as you have a meeting with a film company to talk about a part in the Pete Hope's new film. We also need to talk about three TV projects in the pipeline. Devel, you're hot news, my darling. We're back on track."

"Max, you're so right, I'm back on track and this time it's my track. I was just calling to wish you such a very happy Christmas and there was something else. Now, what was it? Oh, I know. You're fired. No one, and I mean no one, advises Devel Devonshire to do a toilet commercial. Goodbye."

Well, that was that sorted. Now time to prepare for Christmas outfits. I need something for Christmas Day lunch which has to be quite conservative as it's midday. I think the suit I wore in the newspaper interview. New Year's Eve is the time for the film star look, but the problem is what to wear for tomorrow's dinner with David. How will he be dressed? I don't think it will be jeans. I want to look attractive, because he has to fancy me.

David on the other hand was more concerned about his future than what he would be wearing. He knew Devel loved the hotel and Saltmarsh Quay and also that her career was on a downward turn. Perhaps she was going to be the Hotel Manager. The hotel would always be busy if her name was above the door.

Chapter 16

Christmas Eve had arrived after weeks in the planning. This was the week the hotel made lots of money which made up for the quieter winter months. The guests would start to arrive at lunch time and then at four o'clock afternoon tea would be served in the lounge. It was all very relaxed so that people could mingle and chat. It was now only 10.30. David would have loved nothing more than to knock on Devel's door and ask what her intentions for the hotel were, but strangely during the night when he was tossing and turning while trying to sleep, it was not his future giving him a sleepless night, it was the thought that he might never see Devel again. He had become very fond of her.

Annie and her team had cleaned and polished the hotel to within an inch of its life. Everything was now ready. They only needed the guests to check in. In the meantime she was off to help Devel with her last minute Christmas preparations. This seemed very strange to Annie, because as far as she knew Devel was spending the festive week in her suite, so what would need doing?

"Good morning, Annie. How are you today? Very busy, I expect."

"Not too busy, thank you, Devel. In the run up to Christmas, housekeeping in the hotel is very quiet, so we get ahead. It's good because I don't need to be around until lunch time when the guests start to arrive. How can I help you, Devel?"

"Well, Annie, Glenda's given me a list of all the staff in the hotel and I've a little gift for them. I just need to know which would be most suitable."

Annie could not believe the amount of presents which Devel had wrapped and put into four separate piles. She had bought perfume for the women and aftershave for the men, but as the ages of the staff varied, she had bought Elisabeth Arden for the older women and Victoria Beckham for the younger ones. Similarly, with the men, Armani for the older men and David Beckham for the younger ones. The labels had been hand written but just needed to be put on to the appropriate gift.

"Devel, can I just ask something? It's not really any of my business, but I've noticed you've signed all the gift cards from Devel. Is that a wise thing to do?"

"Oh, that was something I needed to talk to you about. You see, Annie, I'm fed up with all the hiding and from tomorrow I want to be a part of the Christmas celebration here at The Saltmarsh Quay. I've been busy sorting my affairs out in the States and I'm ready to be me rather than just Devel, the actress looking for work, or Devel the celebrity who has to been seen at every high profile event in Hollywood. I want to be Devel, the woman who is enjoying her life with or without makeup, Annie.

I'm moving on to the next part of my life and do you know something? I'm so very excited."

Devel went on to explain that she didn't want anyone else to know about this until the next day as in the meantime she needed to have some serious conversations with a few people. From lunchtime on Christmas Day the world would know that Devel Devonshire was celebrating Christmas in Norfolk. She also needed a little help in getting the suite ready as that night she would be having a guest for dinner. It had to look informal, but special. Annie went to get some table linen and flowers, and top of Devel's list, candles with a Christmas fragrance.

"Annie, I want this to be a very special Christmas Eve."

David's morning had turned a little sour. Marcus was on the way and it was urgent as the last thing he wanted to do was travel to the hotel on Christmas Eve.

"Hi, David. We have a problem. The Board are very worried as the publicity from all of this is not going to help the company. The foreign businessman still wants to buy the hotel. It's been explained to him about the staff losing their jobs and the other businesses in Saltmarsh Quays suffering because of the lack of visitors, but he says that would not be a problem as he wants to invest money in the quay and will employ some of the staff in projects around the quay. He has also secretly visited this week, pretending to be a booking agent for foreign business people. Glenda was very helpful and showed him around. She did nothing wrong as she was just doing her job, but he loved the place so much he's increased the price he's willing to pay."

Marcus went on to say that the Board had contacted the American company who wanted to buy the hotel saying that it wasn't for sale and that the suggestions about it being turned into a private home and staff losing jobs had been resolved. However, they insisted on a meeting here in the following week with another offer which would be more appropriate for Saltmarsh Quay. It was something they didn't need, especially between Christmas and the New Year.

"So, David, that's why I'm here. The Board want to know what you think is best for the hotel and more importantly, for the staff. We're a caring company, but we also need to make money."

David was relieved when reception phoned to inform him that the Christmas guests were starting to arrive and he needed to be there to greet them. Marcus understood and left, saying that he would phone David as soon as he knew the date of the Americans' arrival.

Annie made sure the suite was ready for the dinner party while Devel spent most of that time on the phone. From what Annie could hear, it sounded very serious. She really wouldn't want to have been the person on the other end.

"Oh, Annie, it's looking so lovely. Once I light the candles tonight it will be perfect. I think everything's ready. You're so kind and helpful, Annie. Saltmarsh Quay is not just a beautiful, magical place, but the people are some of the nicest people I've ever met. I've just got one more thing to do and that's take that stupid wig out for its last trip to the beach. As from tomorrow it will be no more."

"While you're getting yourself ready, I'll nip to the kitchen and fetch you a flask of hot chocolate. It's not that warm out there today and it will give you some warmth ready for the walk back."

"Thank you so much, Annie. You spoil me. I'm so looking forward to spending time here at Saltmarsh Quay for many years to come."

Annie went to get the hot chocolate, thinking to herself: What does Devel know? If the hotel was to become a private home, she wouldn't be able to come back although I suppose she could rent one of the holiday cottages.

Devel had really wrapped up warm, not forgetting the dreaded wig and glasses. Annie was in reception waiting for her as she came down the stairs. Devel noticed how busy it was, but no one even gave her a second glance.

"There you go, Miss Spring. Hot chocolate and a few of the chef's biscuits. Have a lovely walk."

David was chatting to an elderly couple who came for Christmas every year. They were talking about how the journey took less time because of a new dual carriageway. David could see Devel leaving for her walk.

"David, I'll take over from you now. You've got a busy few days ahead, so why don't you take a break for a couple of hours? Perhaps some fresh air would help. I'm sure there might be someone down on the beach who would like some company."

"Glenda, is it that obvious?"

"Only to us who know you well. I think it's about time you had something else in your life other than this hotel."

"Am I being silly, Glenda? I feel like a teenager."

"Go now, David, or else she'll be on her way back."

As he got to the bottom of the coastal path he could see Devel sitting on the rock. She hadn't seen him, so he could still turn round and go back to the hotel, but he had so many questions for her. For some strange reason, he could not remember any of them as his heart was beating fast. It seemed so stupid, but he loved her. Not the actress in all those films, but the woman who had sat in his cottage and poured her heart out to him."

"Hello, David. It's really cold. Would you like to share my hot chocolate?"

Devel poured more of the hot chocolate into her cup and passed it to David. They both sat there in silence, staring out to sea. David didn't want to speak as he just was so happy to be sitting there with Devel.

"David, that's the magic I'm always talking about. It's in the waves as they break against the beach. The sound is just so special. This little beach is like a drug to me, a drug I don't think I can live without."

Nothing else was said. Neither of them looked at each other as they slowly walked back up the hill to the hotel. David wanted the walk to last forever. He didn't want them to go in separate directions and the last thing in the world he wanted was to have to socialise with the guests, but it was his job. Each and every guest had to be made to feel special.

The hotel was buzzing. Christmas music was playing in the background and the waiting staff were getting everything ready for afternoon tea. A pianist had arrived and was arranging his music. Glenda informed him that there were just four more rooms to check in. Everyone was happy so far. The worst was over with now, he just needed to make sure everyone had a good time.

Once back in her room, Devel checked her emails. None were really important, just the usual 'have a lovely Christmas, we're missing you' messages. What rubbish, she thought, unless you were in a top TV series or a hot new film, no one ever missed you. Reception put a call through to her.

"Hello. Yes, Miss Spring here. Thank you so much, I really appreciate that. You say sixteen properties fit the criteria. That's so helpful. If you could email them to me, I'll get back to you after the holiday. Have a lovely Christmas."

She had ticked everything off her list and now it was time to get herself ready for the evening. She had a long soak in the bath and used some of the nice new moisturiser she had bought. There was no rush, she had plenty of time to pamper herself.

***

The afternoon tea reception was progressing perfectly. The chef and his team had excelled themselves with the cakes, the guests were reuniting with people they had met over the years in the hotel and David, Glenda and Annie mingled, chatting to everyone. This is what made the hotel so successful, not just the friendliness but also the five-star treatment. Christmas had started, but would it be the last Christmas these guests would ever be able to enjoy at The Saltmarsh Cliff Hotel?

Devel had butterflies in her stomach. All she was doing was having dinner with a friend. Well, perhaps dinner with someone she was very fond of. She had changed outfits four times and now returned to the first one she had tried. She lit the candles, making the room look beautiful. Annie had made everything look lovely. The table was simply decorated, but so elegant. Devel poured a small glass of wine and waited for David to arrive.

All the guests were happily enjoying their

champagne reception before going into dinner and the carol singers from Saltmarsh Church were on fine form. The choir master said that it was one of their favourite places to perform. Glenda commented to David that of course it would be as they all look forward to the little buffet laid on for them after the carol singing.

"Ladies and gentlemen, I would just like to say a few words. First of all, I would like to welcome you all to The Saltmarsh Cliff Hotel. My staff and I really hope you have a marvellous Christmas here with us. If there is anything you need, please don't hesitate to ask one of the team. Now there's just one thing for me to say – your Christmas Eve gala dinner is served. Please make your way into the dining room where the restaurant team are waiting to greet you. Have a lovely evening."

David went back to his office and wondered whether he should change his clothes. If there were to be a problem in the hotel he would need to come down and resolve it. He was being silly. All he was doing was going for a meal. It wasn't a date, or was it? Where was the gift he had got for Devel? Should he give it to her today or tomorrow? Oh, pull yourself together, he thought to himself.

Annie had kindly agreed to bring the dinner up to the suite. All she had to do was to wait for Devel to ring down to the kitchen. Surprisingly, even Annie felt nervous. Something told her that this was a very special evening and she was part of it. David stood outside Devel's room and took a deep breath. Here goes, he thought. It's now or never.

"Good evening, David. How's everything going down there?" I heard the carol singers. What a perfect start to Christmas. Can I pour you a glass of champagne?"

"That would be lovely, thank you. Yes, they all seem very happy. Quite a few of the guests have stayed here for Christmas before, so they know each other and it creates a lovely atmosphere. Dinner is being served and later we organise minibuses to take them to Midnight Mass in the local church and back for a hot toddy, before they go to bed and Santa arrives."

"What a lovely way to spend Christmas. I'll just ring down to the kitchen and get our dinner sent up."

"Devel, the suite is looking gorgeous, and the table, how great that looks!"

"I couldn't have made it look so good. This is all down to Annie. What would this hotel do without her, and without you, of course?"

"I know. It's Annie I will worry about the most when the hotel is sold. Since her husband died, the staff have become her family and without them in her life every day, I don't know what she'll do."

"Let's not talk about the hotel tonight. I'm sure everything will come right in the end."

Annie arrived with the dinner in a heated trolley. She wished both of them a happy evening and a lovely Christmas and left them to enjoy their evening. The chef had cooked poached salmon with a selection of vegetables, followed by a raspberry and rhubarb Eaton mess for dessert. They chatted over dinner about some of the Christmases which Devel had celebrated in the States. It was only when she mentioned famous musicians and actors, that it really hit home to David that he was spending Christmas with one of the most famous women in the world.

After dinner David made a quick call down to Glenda to see if everything was going well. Everything was perfect. Everyone was happy and although the last guests had checked in halfway through dinner, they were happy.

"Yes, they're a gay couple and I really think they'll add a lot of sparkle to the Christmas celebrations." There was enough sparkle on the guest's outfits to light up the whole of Saltmarsh Quay!"

As David came off the phone, Devel was reading a text which had just come through and was smiling to herself.

"Sparkle, David? What's sparkling?"

"Oh, the last guests have arrived and Glenda thinks they will light up the Christmas celebrations."

"I'm sure Glenda's right. Let's sit looking out to sea, David."

Devel poured them both another glass of

champagne and handed David a beautifully wrapped little box. The card read – 'Thank you for making my time here in Saltmarsh Quay one of the most special times I've ever had, love Devel. Merry Christmas!' Unwrapping the paper, David found the little box. Carefully opening it, he was surprised to see a watch with an engraving on the back, which read 'With all my love, Devel.' David felt choked. It was so beautiful.

"Thank you so much. You really shouldn't have. It's beautiful. I'm just so happy your stay here has been all right. I realise the reason why you've been with us is different but the treatment you've received here is no different than that of any of the guests who stay. But you're the first guest I've had stay at my cottage and I've never had dinner in one of the suites before."

"I'm so glad you like it. Shopping online is so difficult when you want to buy something special. I was very apprehensive."

They sat there looking out to sea. There were no boats, just the moon shining onto the water and even the sea looked as though it had stopped for Christmas. The waves were still and everything looked so calm.

"Magical, David. That's what this place is. When God created Saltmarsh Quay, he created something very special."

David was so in the moment that he almost forgot to give Devel her present. He finally remembered it and handed it to her.

"I really didn't know what to get you. What do you get one of the most famous women in the world? I really hope you like it."

Devel took the present from David and carefully undid the wrapping. It was a frame of some sort. She had it upside down, but there was something written on the back – 'To Devel, when you look at this, I hope it will remind you of the happy times here at Saltmarsh Quay. All my love, David.' She turned the frame around and there it was, the most stunning painting of the hotel. It took her breath away and she could feel herself welling up.

"Thank you, David. It's beautiful. The artist has captured the building perfectly and to see it with the spring flowers makes it look so much softer."

"I just thought that when you're back in the States it would remind you of the time spent here in England."

There was silence again. Neither of them knew what to say. Devel got up and took the painting over to one of the tables and as she sat back down, she got a little closer to David. She looked at him, turned, moved in towards him and kissed him but didn't move away. David wasn't shocked. This felt so right. He touched her face and their lips touched. Everything was soft and gentle. The butterflies had gone. He wasn't nervous anymore. This was just how it should be. She was not Devel Devonshire, the actress. She was Devel, the woman he was falling in love with.

Suddenly his phone rang. He looked and saw that it was the hotel number.

"I'm so sorry, David. You know I wouldn't disturb you unless it was really urgent, but the lady in Suite 22 has been taken ill. The doctor has called for an ambulance. Would you be able to come to reception?"

David explained the situation to Devel. She understood and he thanked her for a lovely evening and the gift.

"Devel, the hotel will be very busy tomorrow, but I'd like to see you at some point during the day. I don't know when I'll be free. It might be quite late, if that's all right?"

"Yes, that would be nice. I'm sure we'll be able to see each other, and thank you for making this a very special evening for me."

They kissed one more time and David left Devel's suite.

By the time David got to reception the ambulance had arrived and the doctor was telling the driver about the guest. She was going to be all right, but he just wanted her to be checked over. There was nothing David needed to do. The other guests were returning from Midnight Mass, the staff were ready with the hot toddies and that was Christmas Eve over with. David and Glenda handed the hotel over to the night porter and both made their way home.

As David had been drinking, he decided to walk back to the cottage. How he loved this place. He felt so sad that the two things he cared about and really wanted in his life were going to be taken away from him – his beloved hotel and Devel, who would soon be leaving to go back to America. What would the future hold for him? One thing he knew was that never again would he be as happy as this.

Chapter 17

It was a very early start for David as he had given Glenda the day off to spend Christmas Day with her family. Reception would be quiet, as everyone had checked in the day before and no one was leaving for a further three days. He went in to check everything was ready for the breakfast service. The tables looked lovely with gifts on each from the hotel to the guests. The waiting staff were ready to greet the guests, the housekeeping team were arriving and hoping to clean the rooms while the guests were are at breakfast so they could get off early to spend Christmas with their families.

"Morning, David. A very happy Christmas to you."

"Thank you, Annie, and a merry Christmas to you too."

All the departments were ready for a very busy day. Once breakfast was over, it was a mad dash to get the restaurant turned around and looking its very best for the Christmas Day lunch. Annie loved to see everyone dressed up and enjoying a very special meal.

"Oh, Annie, how many years have the two of us stood here on Christmas morning saying how lucky we both are? This is it, the last Christmas we'll both see here."

"Now, David, we can't think like that. We have to

give a hundred percent and most of all enjoy the day. I'm off up with Devel's breakfast tray."

"I was thinking that her day is going to be very lonely up there by herself. I really can't believe she has stayed here for the Christmas period. I thought she would have gone back to the States."

"Somehow I think she'll have a nice day. You just see."

Devel had been up for hours as the UK were eight hours ahead of America. She wanted to get some emails sent to wish friends a happy day before they were up and could return them.

"Good morning, Annie. Can I wish you a very happy Christmas? I have a little gift for you."

"Devel, you shouldn't have! A very merry Christmas to you."

Annie opened the present. Inside a little box was a beautiful locket. When she opened it there was an inscription inside which read, 'To Annie, thank you for your kindness and friendship, with love from Devel'.

"It's so beautiful! I don't know what to say."

"You don't have to say anything. It's just a little token of my appreciation for everything you've done for me."

Devel went on to explain that she needed help getting the suite ready as she had invited two guests for pre-Christmas lunch drinks before she went down to the restaurant.

"I'm very nervous, Annie, but I'm fed up with

hiding. I really want this to be a special Christmas."

Annie cleared away all the dishes from the previous night's dinner while Devel spent the time having breakfast and getting ready. With that there was a knock on the door which Annie answered. It was one of the waiters with a bottle of champagne on ice. Devel had chosen to wear her pale blue Chanel suit and a simple string of pearls.

Breakfast was a great success and everyone wished each other a happy Christmas. As it was a dry, crisp morning a few guests were going for a walk before lunch. David and the restaurant team were organising the room. They had to move the piano in as a pianist would be playing though lunch. The tables were allocated, although some guests had requested to sit together. David went through the lists, putting names on the tables. When he got to Mark and James, it said table for three, but there were only two names. It couldn't be a mistake as Glenda didn't make mistakes. He told the staff to lay the table for three as it was easier to remove a cover than to add one. He didn't think any more about it and continued with his other tasks.

Annie returned to the housekeeping department. Her supervisor had sent all the staff home as quite a few guests had insisted that they didn't need their rooms cleaned. It was Christmas Day and the staff should be at home enjoying the special day with their families. Annie said goodbye to her supervisor and made a pot of tea. There was an hour until lunch was to be served. She found David in the office.

"Thank you, Annie. That's stage one over with. Everyone seemed more than happy. Lunch is always a big hit, so as long as the kitchen team are on form we should sail through it without any hitches."

"Did you have a nice evening? I noticed the present you gave Devel as I was dusting. It's stunning. The hotel looks so different in the spring."

"Yes, I was hoping she'd like it. I really didn't know what to get one of the most famous women in the world, but think it was a hit. Yes, I had a lovely evening. It was very special. Talking of Devel, she's just had a bottle of champagne sent to her room with three glasses. Do you know anything about it?"

"I thought there was something I'd forgotten to do. I'll have to catch up with you later, David. Sorry."

David knew that Annie had made an excuse to leave because she didn't want to lie to him, but more importantly she didn't want to tell him what it was all about.

"Hello, Mark and James. I've missed you both so much. Look at the two of you. You're looking so fabulous. Thank you so much for coming as I really need your help. How was the flight? What do you think of the hotel? Have you seen the view? It changes every five minutes. Is your suite all right?

More importantly, has the facelift made me look twenty-nine?"

"Happy Christmas, Devel. Thank you so much for flying us over to celebrate the holidays with you. Looking at your hair, it doesn't look like I need to do anything to it. You're looking fabulous. Can we sit down and answer one question at a time while you take a breath?"

Neither of them got the chance to answer any of Devel's questions as she went on and on. She wanted to tell them all about her five week stay in England, except that is, about David. Finally, they managed to get a word in, informing her of the latest Hollywood gossip, who was hot and who wasn't, affairs, divorces and everything in between. They finished the champagne. Within an hour, the whole world would know that Devel was in Norfolk celebrating Christmas. One of the guests would surely take a photo and post it on social media, but the good thing was that she would be with her gay hairdresser and his partner rather than a mystery man.

"Come on, boys. It's showtime. How do I look? Is The Saltmarsh Cliff Hotel ready for Devel Devonshire or would they prefer Miss Spring?"

Mark and James led the way down the main staircase. Devel could hear the piano playing, strangely it was a Barbra Streisand number, 'People who need people' rather than a Christmas carol. How true, she thought. When they reached where

Annie was standing, they looked at each other and smiled.

"Miss Devel, you look stunning. Have a lovely lunch."

"Thank you, Annie. I'm sure I will."

David had his back to them and was chatting to two guests as the three of them entered the restaurant. Mark and James stood by the door, waiting for him.

"Hello. Welcome to The Saltmarsh Cliff Hotel. It's so nice of you to join us for the Christmas. I hope everything is okay with your room. Don't hesitate to let us know if there's anything else you require. We have it that you've requested a table for three. Is that correct?"

With that Devel joined them. David was gobsmacked as she looked stunning. All the guests stared in amazement. They could not believe who had just walked in. The pianist stopped playing, stood up and started to clap, followed by applause from all the guests. David led the three of them to their table; Devel, the star, not the Devel David had fallen in love with, smiled. He was as star struck as the rest of them. As he handed them the menu, Devel touched his hand and his whole body tingled as their eyes met.

"Thank you so much, David. Can I introduce you to my hairdresser, Mark and his partner, James? Also, if it's not too much trouble, could I order champagne for everyone?"

"Nice to meet you, David. We've heard a lot about you and your beautiful hotel."

"All good, I hope. I'll go and organise the champagne. Have a lovely lunch."

David was thankful to leave the restaurant to compose himself. He bumped into Annie.

"I think I've got a bone to pick with you."

"Oh, David, you wouldn't have wanted me to spoil the surprise. Doesn't she look beautiful? Now the excitement starts though."

"I know what you mean. The press will be at the door again."

David had organised the champagne, the atmosphere in the restaurant was lovely, but the best thing was that people didn't interrupt Devel during lunch. Annie brought down all the presents which Devel had bought for the staff and once the guests had left the restaurant all the staff on duty sat down and ate their lunch before getting the room ready for the evening gala.

Devel was excited because after the lunch she wanted to show Mark and James the little beach.

"Wrap up warm. Hats, scarves and gloves are essential."

"Devel, do we have to do this today? Can't it wait? We've eaten a huge lunch. The last thing we need is a walk."

"We have to do it today, it's perfect. Let's walk that lunch off. No doubt there'll be someone hiding in the bushes with a camera tomorrow. I can see the headlines already. What's an ageing actress doing in Norfolk? Come on, shake a leg or else it'll be dark."

Devel led the way. Both the boys weren't really dressed for the occasion, but she had told them to come prepared so it was their own fault. She felt good not having to put the disguise on, the itchy wig was no more. Annie had prepared a couple of flasks of hot chocolate and when they finally got to the bottom, Mark and James could both see why Devel loved it so much. It was magical. Nature at its very best.

"Devel, can I say one thing? All the time we've been with you today the one thing you haven't mentioned is your work. The whole point of coming here was to help to get you acting roles. Surely you should be excited about that. Instead all you talk about is Saltmarsh Quay. I know it's stunningly beautiful but it's not exactly busy, and come to that it's not Hollywood."

"Exactly, Mark. It's not Hollywood, and that's what I love so much about it. The peace and quiet, the beauty, it's paradise even on a cold, windy day like today."

"Are you thinking of buying a holiday home here? It's such a long way to travel. There are places like this home in America, quiet little towns, which are just as nice."

"I agree with you, there are, but Saltmarsh Quay has something that nowhere else has. It's got magic.

It draws you in. I've fallen in love with the place so much."

In all the years Mark had known Devel, he had never seen her like this. Going into the restaurant at lunch time was all a game she'd been playing for years, but down here on the beach she was so content. Yes, that's the word. He really felt as though he didn't know her. Not in a bad way, of course. He was just so happy for her.

It was all go back at the hotel. With the staff lunch over, it was time to get ready for the gala. The food was quite straightforward as guests would have had a big lunch. The chef arranges a Christmas gala buffet with a six piece band so everyone can dance; all very relaxed and informal. Devel had no intentions of attending. She had made her appearance for the day and would await the outcome via social media and the press. Her evening would be spent quietly in her suite with Mark and James. David on the other hand would be spending his evening socialising and making sure everything was running perfectly.

David put an answer phone message on the hotel phone saying that the hotel was fully booked until the first week of January and that if anyone had any questions they could email the hotel. That would put pay to all the Devel Devonshire questions. All he had to do now was wait for the reporters to come knocking.

Chapter 18

Home at last and David was so happy to be back in his cottage. Thankfully, Glenda was back from her Christmas break and so he handed the hotel over to her for a few days. It was six o'clock on the day after Boxing Day. All the Christmas celebrations were over and there was just one more event to host – the hotel's New Year's Eve Ball, although there was a couple of days to recover before that. David poured himself a glass of wine and thought to himself: You can stop smiling. There's no one here to please. Just yourself for a couple of days, no more rich food. Cheese on toast, burger and chips; perfect wind down food.

He sat reflecting on the previous days' festivities. All the food services had gone really well, the Christmas Night gala was a major hit, and the Boxing Day treasure hunt and theatre show had really impressed everyone. However, the talking point of the whole Christmas had to be Devel's entrance on Christmas Day. David was sad to think that he hadn't spoken to her since the lunch as she had stayed mostly in her suite with her two friends, but he had been so busy he wouldn't have had time to chat anyway.

Devel was also reflecting on her Christmas. The boys had just left to catch a late flight back to the States. They'd had a fun time, but Devel was in no great hurry to go back to Hollywood with them. Now they'd gone it gave her time to flick through the few press stories about her stay in Norfolk. It had been the not knowing where she was that had caused all the uproar. Now she had outed herself, no one really cared and so it was a bit of a win win situation.

David decided to catch up on his emails for an hour. There wasn't much of any importance, although there was one from Marcus stating a time for the meeting with the American agents who were interested in the hotel. David emailed Glenda the date and time and they required a meeting room for eight people and lunch for nine, which seemed strange. Once he'd organised that, he poured himself another glass of wine. Oh, it was good to be home.

It was very late for Annie to be leaving, but she wanted to clean as many of the free rooms as possible, ready for the New Year's Eve guests. The next days would also be easier as she no longer needed to take care of Devel since everyone knew who she was. Annie thought she ought to check to see if Devel needed anything as she knew that her friends had left.

"Hello, Annie. This is a nice surprise. How are you?"

"I'm fine, thanks. A little tired, but I was wondering if there's anything you needed before I go off duty."

"I don't think so, but to be honest I'm at a bit at a loose end now the boys have gone. It's too cold and dark to go out and I'm not in the mood to go down to the restaurant. Perhaps I'll watch a little television. Is David around the hotel tonight? I'd like to thank him for a lovely Christmas."

"No, I'm afraid he's finished for a few days. I know he has to pop in for a meeting at some point but that's about it until New Year's Eve."

"Oh, has he gone away?"

"No, his last words to me were that he was going home to his cottage, put his smile in the drawer and relax with wine and cheese on toast."

"That sounds lovely."

"Devel, I'm sure he wouldn't say no to some company and I'm driving past his cottage on my way home, if you'd like me to drop you off."

"Annie, really! Do you think he'd mind?"

"Mind? He'd be over the moon to see you, but I hope you like cheese on toast."

Annie gave Devel ten minutes to get herself ready and off they went. Devel kept asking Annie whether she was doing the right thing and Annie laughed and said that if David closed the door on her, she'd drive her back up to the hotel.

"Hello, I'm really sorry to bother you, but I hear you serve the best cheese on toast in the area and I was wondering if you had any to spare. I've brought my own wine, if you'd like to share it with me."

David laughed and they both waved to Annie as

she drove off.

"Come in. If you're lucky you might get some onion with the cheese."

Devel loved this cottage with the aroma of the wood burner and the cosy little rooms. David poured some wine and they sat chatting about Christmas Day lunch and how kind the guests had been towards her. Devel put some music on and then apologised for doing so.

"Don't be silly. Put on whatever music you like. I'll pour us another glass of wine."

As he placed her wine on the side table, he turned towards her and gave her a little kiss.

"Just the one, David? I was expecting more than one."

They giggled and got closer to each other. One kiss led to another and before long, Devel stood up.

"I think we should go upstairs. David, what do think?"

David led the way and for the next four hours they made love and chatted and made love again. They were both so happy. As for the cheese on toast, well that never materialised. The next morning there was no rushing off for David. Coffee was made and they stayed in bed until 11.00 when they had a shower together. Devel's skin was so soft. David had never wanted to touch a woman in the way he wanted to touch her. She was in paradise. He was so gentle and caring and he made her feel so special.

Once up and dressed Devel looked at him and said:

"I'm waiting. Where's my cheese on toast?"

After they ate, Devel said that she needed to make a few phone calls. They had already decided that she'd be staying in the cottage with David for the next couple of days. She had spoken with Annie on the phone and was going to pack a bag of things which Devel would need and then David would go up to the hotel to fetch them.

Devel got on with her calls and checked her emails. She was pleased with all she had achieved and by the time David got back she had finished. On his way back, David stopped at the village shop for more wine and snacks. They were both on a mission not to eat anything healthy. David smiled to himself as he locked the car door. They were like two kids planning a sleepover, yet they weren't kids. They were two very mature adults falling in love and one just happened to be a famous actress.

They spent the next few days talking and laughing about things from their childhood. In fact, everything apart from what they should be talking about, which was Devel's connection to the sale of the hotel, although she was very interested in what the hotel was like before the refurbishment. David showed her photos.

Chapter 19

Devel was up very early as she wanted to walk from the cottage back to the hotel. David had said he would drive her as it was still dark and very cold, but she needed to be by herself to think things through. It was going to be a long day ahead and after what David had said the previous evening, Devel realised it was up to her to win the deal.

David didn't have to be at the hotel for several hours as Marcus wasn't arriving until 11.00. He started to think about the last few days and could not recall a time when he had ever felt so happy. He just didn't want this little bubble to burst and somehow he got the feeling that it wasn't going to. Devel wanted the hotel and no one was going to stand in her way.

Devel showered and put on a smart suit. This was business. She didn't normally need to put the showbiz smile on for meetings. Max would have done all the talking, but he was in the past and as she didn't have a manager she would have to up her game. Her first meeting of the day was with her solicitor and accountant who had flown over from the States the day before. They had studied all the paperwork supplied by the hotel and they could see that it was a very profitable business and the company had a genuine reason for selling it.

"Devel, first of all, are you sure you really want

to do this? Money is not the issue. With what Malcolm left you, there's more than enough to cover the purchase and to be honest, you don't need to make money out of the hotel. That said, you shouldn't lose any either. We both want to make sure you're doing the right thing for you."

"Thank you both. I know if you had any doubts that I was doing the wrong thing, you wouldn't let me go ahead with it. It's not so much about wanting to own a hotel, but more about living somewhere I love and giving a future to the people of Saltmarsh Quay. That won't happen unless the other people pull out."

They went over a lot of paperwork. Devel's accountant explained the things to her which Max used to deal with. Did she really need an agent? Her accountant had looked after her affairs for years, so nothing needed to change. The phone rang and Devel answered it.

"Thank you, Glenda. Could you send them up in ten minutes? I think I'll do this by myself if that's all right. With three of them against me, they'll think they're in for an easy ride, but they don't know who they're coming to see yet."

"It's so good of you to come and see me. Please come in and take a seat."

"Aren't you...?"

"Yes, that's right. I'm Devel Devonshire. Can I get you some refreshments? Tea? Coffee? Water?"

The three agents were gobsmacked. They had

thought they were coming to deal with sharp talking businessmen, but instead here was this famous actress. It threw them completely and before they could open their mouths to speak, Devel was ready with her pitch.

"The situation is quite simple. I want to buy this hotel and you want it for your client. I understand that this is the only property you've found which fits your client's criteria. Well, I think perhaps you've been rather lazy. Yes, lazy is the word because I've found quite a few. I stopped at twelve but I'm sure my agent could have found dozens more. So what do we do about this little problem? Do you tell your client about these other properties or do I tell him? By the way, four of the houses there in front of you fulfil all his needs, unlike this one as it doesn't have a helicopter pad and garages for twelve cars."

Devel could see how uncomfortable they felt so she suggested that perhaps they needed some time to talk about the situation and explained there was a meeting room available for them to use. She thanked them for their time and suggested they take with them the information about the other properties.

"Lead the way, David. Where are they? We need to put a stop to this."

David showed the directors into another meeting room and introduced them to the other interested parties. Marcus explained they had done a deal and in just a matter of days they would be selling the hotel to a private buyer. The only reason they had come today was out of politeness, seeing that they had travelled all the way from the States.

"We really appreciate you seeing us, but our client really wants to purchase this hotel and they feel it would be far more beneficial for Saltmarsh Quay community if you sold it to them."

David just wanted the ground to open up. He'd never seen Marcus as worked up as this before. Marcus went on to explain the concerns of the company, but the businessman hoping to buy it would be investing very heavily in the quay and offering employment to local people on several projects. This debate continued for half an hour. The Americans were becoming slightly worried as they knew how much Devel wanted the hotel and they really didn't know how to get it for her.

David tried his best to lighten the atmosphere and suggested it was time for lunch although he wasn't sure about who was joining them? Obviously it must be Devel, but this left one place. He led the way into the private dining room and as it was a circular table, everyone could see each other very clearly. He did think he should have told the directors that Devel was the mystery buyer. Oh, to hell with it. He knew that whatever the outcome, his relationship with Devel would continue.

They had just seated themselves when the door opened and in walked Devel. Marcus and the two directors were stunned and did not know what to say.

"Hello, it's so lovely to meet you all. I'm very sorry to drag you away from your Christmas break but I felt this all had to be resolved before we go in to a New Year. If you don't know who I am, I'm Devel Devonshire and I've been staying here for several weeks. I've fallen in love with the hotel and the beautiful Saltmarsh Quay and want to buy it. However, you seem to want to sell it to someone else so we are at a bit of a stalemate. If you could just bear with me a moment, I've invited someone to join us for lunch. He won't be a minute, he's just having a chat to the agents that you're dealing with."

There was a knock at the door and in walked a very tall and handsome man.

"Can I introduce you to Hank Keeley Jnr? I thought that seeing he's the other potential buyer for the hotel, it would be a good idea to thrash this out over lunch."

Marcus and the directors were so uncomfortable with the shock of the world famous actress Devel being there as well as one of the top American billionaires. All they had wanted to do was sell the hotel, which should have been quite a straightforward procedure. Lunch was served and Devel explained that ever since she had been able to find out the identity of the other buyer, they had been in contact with each other.

"You see, gentlemen, the agents I instructed to

find a home for myself and my family really didn't do a good job. As Devel wants to buy this one, she instructed another agent to find something more suitable for me and managed to find me some beautiful houses, mansions and even a mini castle to view so the outcome is—"

David was feeling relieved, sick and exhausted, but thankfully Devel was getting the hotel.

"Devel, you are one of the finest actresses the world has ever seen and I say it myself, I'm a bloody good business man and I thank you so much for all the hard work you've put into finding a property for me, but... yes there's a but, and that is I'm still going to buy this hotel. The other properties might suit my needs better, but like you. I've fallen in love with Saltmarsh Quay."

No one wanted to look at Devel. The room was so tense but someone had to speak. They all sipped water and fiddled with napkins. David kept thinking to himself: Speak someone. Bloody well say something.

"Oh, Hank, I'm bitterly disappointed. I do understand more than anyone the attraction you have for the hotel and the quay, but there's just one thing I would like your thoughts on, if you don't mind."

They were getting even more uncomfortable and David noticed that even Hank was a little nervous.

"What would that be, Devel?"

"It's such a beautiful space and obviously you'll

be entertaining a lot of top American politicians here. You never know, one day you might even have an American President to stay, but I was wondering how you'd get around the little problem of security. As you well know, the UK is quite a small island and all the way around it there is a coastal path. Here at the hotel, the path goes right through the grounds. Anyone can walk on the path. It gives beautiful views out to sea, but people can also look right into this property. Ever since the property was built, people have tried to reroute the path and every time they've failed due to the British government refusing permission."

Yes, Devel had played a trump card. David wanted to laugh out loud, but he could see from Hank's face that he was not a happy man. He looked at both Marcus and the directors.

"Is this true? Why wasn't this ever pointed out before? I need complete privacy and security for my family and friends?"

Marcus went on to explain that it had all been discussed with the agents and that he was sure it had also been confirmed in emails.

"Well, Devel, it looks like you've got yourself a hotel. There's no way I'm going to ruin my reputation by fighting the British government and losing. You're not just a fabulous actress, but a very clever businesswoman. I take my hat off to you. Just one thing, Devel, but would my family and I be welcome to come and stay from time to time?"

"Thanks. You would be more than welcome and please, your first visit would be free of charge."

Chapter 20

Four hours later, David and Devel were sitting up in bed at the cottage drinking champagne and reliving the events of the lunch. Apparently, Marcus had said to David afterwards that if he had known all the fuss it would cause, he would have asked more money for the hotel. However, both he and the other directors left happy. As for the agents, I don't think Hank would be employing them again. Devel was feeling very chuffed with herself and rightly so, as taking on someone as powerful as Hank took a lot of guts.

"The only reason I knew it would be a problem for him was because my solicitor kept pointing it out to me. Yes, if I was buying it as my home I probably would have thought twice, but seeing as it's a hotel, that's different. Talking of my home, I think I might need a little help from someone who knows the area very well. As much as I love the hotel, I don't actually want to live in it full time. I was wondering whether there were any houses for sale down on the quay. Not too big, four or five bedrooms and a little garden, but saying that, if I asked nicely, that lovely hotel manager might let me stay in his cottage for the odd night. What do you think?"

They did not stop giggling but they had to admit then that making love was so special for both of them.

The next morning they were up early. It was New Year's Eve and a very busy day for the hotel. David and Devel had both decided it was the perfect occasion to tell the staff the exciting news. Devel had suggested that all the staff should be invited to the hotel to celebrate the New Year and they could have a little buffet and drinks in one of the function rooms. Neither of them thought it was right to let them mix with the paying guests and that after midnight they could come into the large restaurant and be told all the news.

Back at the hotel David got on with checking everything with all his Heads of Department. Devel had asked him if she could tell Annie and Glenda herself, which David didn't consider to be a problem. Everything was happening very fast. Devel had obviously just taken it for granted that David would still manage the hotel but that might be awkward. However, it wasn't the day to be worrying about it. They should just welcome in the New Year and see what it had to offer in the future.

The hotel was ready. Most of the guests had checked in and David had personally welcomed them all. Devel broke the news to Glenda and Annie and then Annie helped Devel choose something nice to wear. The staff and their partners were excited to be going up to the hotel to welcome in the New Year, the band had arrived and were setting up. There was just time for David to pop up to see

Devel before dinner was served.

"Are you really sure you're doing the right thing? Do you want the responsibility of owning a hotel in a country you're not that familiar with? It's not too late to change your mind, Devel, as nothing's been signed yet."

"Do you really think I'd go to all this trouble if I didn't know whether I was doing the right thing? Come on, David, in the short time you've known me I'm sure you've sussed me out better than that. Now come on, let's get the party started. Well, let you get the party going! I'll come down after the dinner's finished. One grand entrance a year is enough. This time I'll slip in very quietly later."

They kissed goodbye and told each other how happy they both were. As David closed Devel's door behind him, she laughed as she heard him shout "Show time."

Chapter 21

It was one of the biggest nights of the year for the hotel and as well as the residents, the locals from Saltmarsh Quay were all excited to be celebrating New Year's Eve. As David walked in the reception, the staff were welcoming guests with glasses of champagne. Everyone had really gone to town on their outfits. The men were all in dinner suits and as for the ladies, sparkles were an understatement with their beautiful evening dresses. The band was playing in the background and the chef and his team were ready to go with a mouth-watering five-course dinner. The atmosphere was building and it looked like it would be a very special evening.

"Ladies and gentlemen. My name's David Rose, and I'm the Manager of the The Saltmarsh Cliff. I and my team would like to welcome you to this very special evening here at the hotel. If you would like to make your way through to the restaurant, we will shortly be serving our celebrated New Year's Eve dinner."

The band played throughout the dinner. David walked from table to table, checking everything was in order. Several of the guests asked whether Devel would be joining in the celebration. David smiled and said that he thought that Devel would be coming down from her suite later. Once the waiting staff had served coffee, David called them into the kitchen. Standing beside him were three men, all dressed smartly in waiter uniforms.

"Could I just have a little quiet please? I have a little surprise for you. As a huge thank you, I've got these three young men from a catering agency to come and serve drinks and look after our lovely guests for the rest of the evening. So once the coffee is cleared away and the room is ready for the dancing, I'm giving you all the evening off to welcome the New Year in with your colleagues in the meeting rooms. Thank you to Chef for putting a last minute buffet together for the staff. Please have a lovely evening and thank you again. Oh, just one more thing. I would like you all to come into the ballroom at midnight to welcome in the New Year.

Devel had spent the last few hours getting ready. She could hear the band playing and poured herself another glass of champagne while looking out to sea. It was pitch black without any boats on the horizon and as it was a cloudy night, the moon wasn't very bright. Oh, Devel, you're so lucky, she thought. After all these years of working non-stop trying to please fans, film companies and management, this is a new start and there couldn't have been a better night of the year to be starting it. Her black evening dress was hanging up, ready to wear. She stared at it and thought to herself that perhaps it might be slightly understated as it was a special night for both her and the hotel.

The staff rushed around clearing dirty glasses

and coffee cups from the tables, the lights were dimmed and two singers had joined the band. The agency barmen were ready to go and it was time to start the celebrations in earnest.

"Ladies and gentlemen, I hope you've all enjoyed the dinner. It's now time for me to hand the rest of the evening over to Ken and his marvellous band and singers, who will entertain us with everything from Sinatra to Lady Gaga. Please have a fabulous evening."

The singers began to sing, and people headed to the dance floor. The room was buzzing and lots of the locals started to ask David about the hotel sale. Would he be staying and how would it affect the quay? He reassured them and thought everything would be all right.

"Glenda, could you just keep an eye on things? I'm popping into my office for a few minutes of peace and quiet. Call me if you need me."

David stood at this office window looking out to sea. He still didn't really know where he featured in Devel's plans, but he wasn't worried. His stressful days were over as he was on a different road now, not by himself but with a woman who he was falling in love with and who he believed was falling in love with him. With that, there was a knock at the door.

"Hello, Annie. You look lovely. How's everything going with the little staff party? Have many turned up."

"Yes, everyone's here. They know they can have

fun, but realise they have to keep the noise down and behave themselves. It's such a lovely evening, David, and more importantly a new start for the hotel. I'm so happy for you. Devel's such a lovely person. She's not a diva, just a thoughtful lady who cares for people, but most of all, I think the two of you make a lovely couple."

"Thank you, Annie. I'm very fond of her, but I don't really know what I'm getting myself into. However, I'm excited, and the thing is I've realised that none of us know what lies ahead, so it's important to enjoy the moment and that's just what I'm going to do. Let's go and join the party, Annie."

"Yes, but aren't you missing something, David?"

"I don't know what you mean."

"I think there should be someone on your arm, don't you?"

David got to the top of the stairs, took a deep breath and knocked on Devel's door. She called out for him to enter and he went in to find her in a most beautiful red dress and standing looking out to sea. She was one of the most famous women in the world, yet he was not blown away by her stardom but in awe of the woman who he was falling in love with. She turned around and they smiled at each other.

"Don't you look handsome in your dinner suit?"

"Devel, you look so beautiful. I think we should go and show you off to the lovely people downstairs."

David led Devel down to the party, the band could see her coming and went into their version of the famous song, 'Hello Dolly' which made everyone turn their heads. There was no doubting that she was a true star who appreciated every last bit of the affection she was shown. David stood back and let the guests greet her. He felt so proud of her, the hotel, and for once in his life he was proud of himself.

It was now 11.45 and all the staff had quietly come into the ballroom. David got up on to the stage with the band.

"It's nearly midnight and before we welcome in the New Year, I'd just like to say a few words please. Over the next few weeks there's going to be a few changes here at the hotel. They're very exciting changes as the hotel is going to be sold and it gives me so much pleasure to introduce you to the new owner. Ladies, gentlemen and staff, I give you the owner of The Saltmarsh Cliff Hotel, Devel Devonshire."

Everyone cheered and applauded as Devel took to the stage. As David handed her the microphone she kissed him on the cheek and when the applause had died down, she took a deep breath.

"Thank you so much for that lovely welcome. First of all, I'm so excited to be part of this lovely hotel and especially to be part of the team here. This is the best hotel team in the world. I didn't come here with a view to buy the hotel, but it needed rescuing as someone was going to purchase it for their private home. That would have meant that myself, and all you lovely people, would never have been able to come and stay here again. I had to do something and I'm very fortunate to be in a position to do that. Please don't worry. I'm not going to make any changes to the hotel. It will remain a hotel which you'll all love coming to. That said, hopefully there might be one little change."

There was silence and the staff started to look at each other. David felt his heart beat faster. What changes did she want to make and why hadn't she discussed things with him?

"It's not just the hotel and the beautiful Saltmarsh Quay I've fallen in love with since I've been here in the UK. I've met a man who has become very special to me. He loves me for being me and not Devel Devonshire the actress, and I want to spend the rest of my life with him. So, I've asked Glenda to take over some of the responsibilities of running The Saltmarsh Cliff and she has kindly agreed."

Devel turned towards David, who had turned as white as a sheet and was completely astounded.

"On this very special night for myself and for the hotel, there's something I want to do with every breath in my body and that is to ask David Rose, 'will you marry me?"

THE END

Printed in Great Britain
by Amazon